COURIER'S FIST

COURIER'S FIST

Harvey A. Eysman

BEAUFORT BOOKS, INC.

New York / *Toronto*

Copyright © 1981 by Harvey A. Eysman

Library of Congress Cataloging in Publication Data

Eysman, Harvey A.
Courier's fist.

I. Title.
PS3555.Y7C6 1981   813'.54   80-27338
ISBN 0-8253-0034-7

Published in the United States of America by Beaufort Books, Inc.,
New York. Published simultaneously in Canada by Nelson,
Foster and Scott Ltd.

Printed in the U.S.A.
First Edition
10   9   8   7   6   5   4   3   2   1

To Donna—for her unselfish
and enthusiastic encouragement

February, 1979

The two men sat facing each other. The tall man was ill t ease, his eyes downcast. The shorter man was emotionless, nd looked directly ahead. Several minutes had passed in rained silence, and the room was getting darker.

"How long have you known?" the tall man asked.

"Over ten years," the shorter man said. "Ever since Paris. ine had given you a black book; you never gave it in." There as another long pause.

"Why did you wait so long?"

"You've been feeding the Ruskies hype for ten years; ey've found out. We have no further use for you."

"What do you plan to do with me now?"

"We haven't decided." Rising, the shorter man sighed and alked to the window. It was snowing heavily. "Perhaps we'll ve you back to them."

9

"I'm not a well man, you know," the other replied.

The shorter man said nothing. He watched the floati whiteness turn black as it fell past the headlights of a passir automobile. The tall man withdrew a revolver from his be clip. He placed the barrel in his mouth and blew the back his head off.

October, 1966

1

It was raining. An occasional blast of wind machine-gunned the window of the small office overlooking Sixth Avenue and Forty-second Street. A fat man stood at the window, looking out at the shiny pavement. He was wearing an immaculately cut dark blue suit that made him look prosperous, if not slimmer. Every few minutes he ran his finger down the glass pane in the trail of a raindrop, careful that the cuffs of his white silk shirt not touch the smudged window glass. Impatiently, he turned to the two seated men, and grimaced.

The room was small and dusty. It gave an impression of disuse; the law books that lined one wall were also coated with dust. The small desk behind which the fat man waited was bare, except for a telephone and a small heap of files that lay in a corner. There were two envelopes in the center of the desk, placed there by the fat man, after removing them from the door slot. Facing the desk were two deep, red leather arm chairs, that may have looked expensive at one time, but were now faded and sagging with age. Next to one of them was a small table with some outdated copies of *Life* cluttering the top. The leather desk chair was deep and hard-backed; it looked uncomfortable. In another corner were two filing cabinets.

The other two men were sitting in the leather chairs, one leafing through an old copy of *Life*, the other watching, first the fat man, then the telephone. It had not rung since they had arrived, three hours earlier. From time to time, an elevator in the hall ground to a stop, its metal gate clanked open then shut, and footsteps sounded and ultimately faded away. On each such occasion, the fat man looked up with renewed interest. The other two men remained expressionless.

The fat man turned away from the window, looked at the book-lined wall, and ambled towards it. Carefully, to avoid soiling his cuffs, he removed one of the books from its dusty slot on the shelf. As he did so, the elevator again repeated its ritual. This time footsteps approached the door of the office. A key grated in the lock, and the book slipped from the fat man's hand, falling to the hardwood floor; it made an unreasonably loud noise in the barren room.

The platform of the Canal Street BMT was crowded although the afternoon rush hour had not yet begun. The tunnel shook and clattered in protest, as the train screeched to a stop. Mark Pine entered too late to get a seat, and resigned himself to standing in the small puddle made by the drippings from his black plastic raincoat. He had made fifty dollars that afternoon in Court. The case would have been lost were it not for the settlement, and the fee would pay his two-month overdue phone bill, if not his overdue rent.

Pine detrained at Times Square, and walked to his office,

attempting to shield his face from the driving rain. The building had a decaying odor, as if cats were living in the stairwells, and the elderly elevator operator had egg smeared on the lapel of his gray, washed-out work uniform. The cage opened at his floor, and Pine paced down the hall towards his office. He could see that there was no mail stuck in the door slot. As soon as he had placed the key in the lock, however, he knew that someone was inside. There was a sharp retort, as if a book had been dropped.

Standing in the doorway, Pine saw the fat man first, then the other two. Looking at his desk, he saw two envelopes resting at its center. Nobody said anything as Pine went to the desk and absently looked at the return addresses on the envelopes before turning to the men who had been waiting for him.

"The door was locked," he said.

Neither seated man replied, while the fat man picked up the fallen book, and replaced it in the neat slot from which it had been plucked.

"Do you mind telling me what you're doing here?" Pine added, feeling rather foolish.

"Don't be upset, Mr. Pine," the man with the magazine said, placing the copy of *Life* back on the table. "We had to see you, and your door was locked. It was easier to slip the lock and wait inside, than to stand in that unpleasant hallway. We had almost given up hope of your coming today. I am Percy Diver," he continued, "and my associates are Rudolph King and Mr. Bigger, Charles Bigger," he said, indicating the fat man, with a humorous grin.

Pine wished that the fat man would stop pressing the creases of his pants between his fingers. His actions reminded Pine of a large monkey picking ticks off its body; his first impression that the fat man was immaculate had altered, and he now felt that, under his expensive suits, Bigger wore dirty underwear.

15

"We've come up from Washington to see you," Diver continued, flashing a slim leather case with an ornate card displayed in the window. The card could have been a membership in Alcoholics Anonymous for all Pine could see. "Ever since your discharge from the Marines, Mr. Pine, your records have been in our offices. We could use your help now. The job would pay well, and wouldn't take too much of your time."

"How well, and what's the job?" Pine asked.

"Five grand," Diver said. Pine tried to keep his face expressionless. It was a lot of money, and he needed it badly, but he wondered what the *quo* might be for so much *quid*.

"Whom exactly am I expected to murder, rape, or otherwise dismember?" he said.

"It's nothing like that," Diver replied with a wide grin. "We're with the State Department. We need someone to pick up some papers for us in Paris, and deliver them to the Embassy. That's all."

"Why do you need *me*, and how come such an easy job pays so well?" Pine asked, half afraid that he would talk them out of it.

"Our usual couriers become rather well-known," Diver continued, "and the information we seek is rather sensitive. We can't take a chance on its being intercepted. Your danger will be slight, because you're unknown, and once you make delivery, you can return home."

"Another reason the fee is so high," Diver added, "is that we don't know exactly how long it will take you to make contact with our Paris agent, and you may be stuck there for a few weeks, or even longer. You'll probably have to make arrangements to have your office looked after while you're gone, and of course, you'll have expenses while you are in Paris."

"Do I get a number, like 007, or something?" he asked with

a touch of sarcasm. The fat man tittered in a high rattly voice. "It's not that kind of job, actually," he said. "What we need is a courier, and your name popped out of our files this time. You must realize that we do this frequently, but since we can never use a nonprofessional more than once—it's too dangerous for him and for us—we use a great many civilians over the years. Our best source of names comes from military records."

"I see," Pine said. "You mean, that all I have to do is pick up some papers and bring them to the Embassy in Paris. No shooting, no fights, no homburgs, or trench coats?"

"Really, Mr. Pine," Bigger piped. "It's not a joke."

"Well, it still seems to me that five grand is a lot of money for something as simple as you claim. Look, don't get me wrong. I'm more than happy to take your money, but I would just like to know what I'm getting into."

"You're concerned about why we're paying so much. Is that it?" King said.

"You might say," Pine answered. The other men looked at each other briefly.

"In most cases, we don't pay anything," Diver explained. "Except expenses, that is. In this case, because of the possibility that you may be away for awhile, which could cost you business, we're willing to make a settlement. Also," he paused slightly, "there could possibly be a minor problem or two. Because of the nature of the intelligence, our agent in Paris could be in some danger. We don't expect it to flow over to you since you're a completely unknown element, but the slight risk is worth something. We selected you because of your Marine background, which placed you into our file. Besides," he added grinning, "you were an instructor in hand-to-hand combat, weren't you?"

"If you're willing to take on the assignment, we'll make the arrangements and contact you during the next few days," said King.

17

Pine felt that he was being rushed into something. There was a sense of noncontrol, as if he were in a dream and events were passing over his head, without giving him an opportunity to react effectively.

"Look," he said. "Why can't I have a few days to think it over? It's tempting because the money is more than I make in a year, but I don't like being pushed like this."

King glanced at Diver and smiled.

"We said we would be back to you in a few days," King replied. "If you're willing at that time, let us know then. If not," he paused for a moment and looked down at the edge of the nail on his left index finger. "If not, we'll find someone else. Don't worry."

King's nonchalance made Pine nervous and made the offer even more tempting.

"If you decide to help us," Diver continued, "the money will be deposited directly into your business account. You should plan on an absence of about two weeks."

Pine was standing behind the desk as the three men left the office. He remained standing for a few minutes, thinking only of the money he so badly needed.

2

When Pine had graduated from M.I.T. in 1954, he had been sure of only one thing—he did not like engineering. Tech was a tough place, and tended to engender a dislike for technology in some students, regardless how well they had acquitted themselves during the four years of undergraduate study. Pine had needed only three to graduate, but it was enough to turn him away from the sciences as a profession.

Not knowing what he wanted, he had enlisted in the Marine Corps, and after a rather uninspiring four years, decided to study law. His law school career was less distinguished than his engineering days had been, perhaps because he had been required to clerk his way through, but he had developed an interest in the Law, and after admission to the bar, he began a small practice with the six thousand dollars he had managed to accumulate. His funds had not lasted as long as he had hoped, and now, after too many years of deprivation, he was contemplating closing shop for lack of funds. Diver's offer was a transfusion, even if he suspected that he was getting into more than he should. Sweeping his raincoat from the hook near his desk, he switched off the lights and locked up for the night.

Pine stepped from the building into the now crowded pedestrian traffic. The rain had stopped and he walked across the street to a cheap restaurant, where he could get a steak and a baked potato for a dollar twenty-nine. He thought for a moment about his last and only other trip to Paris, when, as a student, he had spent several months living with a wealthy French widow of tender age and of tender heart. It was the only time that he had ever lived in true luxury.

Pine was a romantic. The prospect of a Parisian adventure, notwithstanding the fortune that was being offered, would under most conditions, have been enough to propel him to the airport. But the nagging alarm that rang somewhere deep within him stayed action and decision. He felt that something was missing from King's explanation and that what was missing was more important than what had been stated. He also knew that as soon as the offer had been made, he was lost; and he was sure that King, Diver, and Bigger had also known that he could not refuse the offer.

The next four days were spent in anxious anticipation; anxious that Diver would not call; anticipation of the adventure before him. A phone had been connected between his office and the lawyer's office next door; his most recent *inamorata* had been advised of his impending departure; he had obtained a vaccination. With the details completed, Pine awaited the call that meant, at least, temporary release from his financial worries. When it finally came, he had all but given up hope of ever again hearing from the three men.

"Mr. Pine," the caller said. "It's King. We're all set on this end. How about you?"

"I'm ready." Pine hoped that his voice sounded more confident than he felt.

"Good," King said. "A man will deliver a ticket and some papers to your office this afternoon. Your money will also be deposited today. Any other questions?"

"Any questions? I got about ten thousand of them. What am I supposed to do, for one?"

"That will be clear in the papers we're sending over. We probably won't see you again, so good luck," King said.

The connection was broken. Pine sat there feeling like a mail clerk who had just been asked to run a Board of Directors meeting. For five grand, Pine thought, somehow they'll let me know what to do.

Thirty minutes later, a disreputable-looking messenger appeared at his door with a large brown envelope in hand.

"Is that for me?"

"Your name Pine?"

"Yeah," Pine said.

"Sign here," the man said, and left without further stimulating conversation.

Pine returned to his desk and opened the envelope. He noticed that it had not been sealed with the mucilage, but only with the pin that had been splayed at the top flap; it seemed a rather sloppy way to conduct a business that he presumed to be so "sensitive." The envelope contained an airline ticket for the next evening at nine o'clock, New York to Paris to open date. The accomodations were tourist class. A letter under the letterhead of Thin Set Pants Co., Inc., at an address on West Thirty-Eighth Street, read:

Dear Mr. Pine:

Please see Mr. Georges Deplint at 9 Rue de Vaugirard, Paris, Apt. 33. Deliver his contracts as per our conversation.

Very truly yours,
R. King

RK:cz

There was also a passport and five hundred dollars in cash. Paper-clipped to the letter was a three-by-five card with the notation: "Candide Hotel, 7 Ave M. le Prince; one room, with bath and toilet, no meals, maid service, 23, 50NF/d; in name Mark Pine from 13/10/66 to open."

Pine reread the letter slowly. It seemed clear and rather simple; that worried him. They even remembered to enclose what appeared to be expense money, as if they knew how little Pine had in his own account. No doubt they did.

The next day, Pine called his bank to see if the five thousand dollars had actually been deposited. He was advised that his account contained exactly four thousand five hundred thirty-three dollars and forty-nine cents. They had taken the five hundred dollars cash, out of his fees.

Kennedy Airport was crowded despite the late hour, and Pine was glad, after waiting at the bar for an hour, to board the plane. Sitting on the aisle, he placed his briefcase on the next seat. His eyes must have closed for a moment, for when next he looked up, a tall blond girl was standing over him. She seemed flustered when he arose to let her in.

Although she was attractive in a lanky way, he was too involved in his own thoughts to take much notice. He did notice that her legs were unquestionably long enough; her skirt was unquestionably not. The plane departed on schedule, the pilot announcing that they would be arriving at Orly at nine the next morning, Paris time. Pine decided to get some sleep.

He slept until shortly before arriving, when the stewardess awakened him for breakfast. The plane landed at 9:14 A.M., and feeling fresh after his sleep, he debarked full of enthusiasm.

3

The Hotel Candide was shabby, but possessed an air of sometime grandeur. The clerk complimented him on his French, but refused to speak with him in anything but English. He was rather supercilious, but Pine had found that most Frenchmen were that way, and it did not bother him more than usual. He was shown to his room by a surly bellhop, who did not say *merci* when given an excessive tip. Trying the bed for size, Pine lay back to compose his plans for the day. He decided to tend to business first, and then to return to some of the places that he remembered from his last trip.

The address to which he was required to go, was only a block or so away, and he regretted its proximity, as he would have liked to have walked a bit. It still bothered him that so large a fee had been paid for so apparently simple a task, but he was not about to complain. The building that bore the correct number, was one of those old French store-dwellings, which must have housed a ground floor shop with living space above it in some earlier age. The paint had flaked off the front, and the windows were filthy, contrasting with the clean stone facings of adjoining commercial buildings, a product of Paris's recent "clean-up" campaign. The darkened stairway sagged threateningly at each step, as he ascended the six storeys to a door marked "33" in large ceramic letters.

Pine knocked softly at first, and then louder after a few moments of silence. His first reaction was annoyance that nobody was there; but, considering that Deplint probably had more to do than wait around for him, he calmed down, and decided to try the door. Finding it open, he entered boldly, reflecting upon the rude manner in which he had met Diver and company.

The room was absolutely the smallest he had ever seen, even in his student days. It could not have been more than four and some feet across and nine feet long. There was a traditionally French window at one end of the room, double casements opening out, constructed of now badly cracked and paint-peeled wood with large panes of gray glass through which he could barely see the smutty backs of the buildings across the way. The rest of the room was equally unprepossessing. A bed, too narrow; a chest of drawers, too shallow; a cabinet for clothing, too short. At the far end of the room was a small sink. On the wall over the bed was an unpainted wooden shelf, nailed crudely into the wall. Opposite that, on the other wall, was a Bonnard print, a nude, upon which someone had added an obscene sketch. But there were no clothes in the cabinet, nor in the drawers, and nothing on the shelves. Even the sink stains were at least a few days old. The room was obviously untenanted.

Feeling somewhat abashed, Pine decided to return later to see if anyone was waiting for him. He was annoyed that he would not be able to make other plans until he had taken care of this business, and there was no way for him to know when he was going to be able to do that; it all depended upon Deplint, if he ever showed up. While he was musing, the door opened behind him and Pine turned, having been startled half out of his skin. A beautiful, but worn blond was standing at the entrance. She came in and closed the door.

"Who are you?" Pine asked.

"It's not important my name," she said with a heavy and not unattractive French accent. "You look for my brother, no?"

"Yes, if he is Monsieur Deplint," Pine said.

"Well, he is dead since two days, and I am waiting for you to come here. He told me," she explained.

"How did you know, er, you said he was dead?" Pine found himself at a loss with this woman; she showed no emotion about her brother, and she had a cold edge to her that he acutely felt.

"You are the American, no? My brother he had information for you, yes? I give it to you from him." She seemed to be getting impatient.

"How did your brother die?" Pine asked.

"His neck, it was cut open."

"Well, who did it? Do you know?" Pine was appalled.

"The men who kill my brother are German. This I know because I see them do it and I recognize one from Dachau." As she said this she pulled up her right sleeve and showed him the blue numerals on her wrist. He had not thought that she was that old.

"I'm terribly sorry Miss," Pine stammered, "but if you have something for me, I'd like to take it and get out of here." He had begun to get the feeling that if Deplint could get it in the neck, so could he. Pine had become a lawyer because he could not stand the sight of blood; he was particularly sensitive about his own. "Is there anything I can tell my people for you?"

"No, there is nothing." She pronounced "nothing" as if it

were two words. Taking a small envelope from her purse, she kept it out of his reach.

"The money you promised my brother; where is it?"

"I didn't know he was to get anything from me," Pine said, wondering for a moment if the five hundred was supposed to be used for this purpose. But he immediately discarded the idea, as he was sure that Deplint had been on a payroll, and he had not been told to make any payoff by Diver.

"One thousand dollars American, please," she demanded, "or you get nothing."

"I wasn't told to give your brother anything. He was supposed to give me, what I presume is in that envelope, and he died for it. So how about being a good little sister, and handing it over."

"My brother was a bastard! It was he what turn me over to the gestapo in the war, so he can have a car to get away."

"Look, lady, I don't give a damn about that now. I have a job to do. Are you going to give me the papers or do I have to take them from you?" Pine was getting tired of the repartee. Suddenly she withdrew a rather small, but deadly looking pistol, which took all the bravado from Pine.

"If you touch me, I will kill you dead," she threatened.

"Now don't point that thing at me lady," he said. "I'm not going to hurt you." He was not quite sure how reactive she might be, but with the gun in her hand, he did not want to push her too far.

"I don't have that kind of money on me," he continued, becoming more upset by the wild look in her eyes. "I was never even told that I had to give your brother anything for the information." Pine made a scramble for the cash he had in his pocket to prove his point, withdrawing the few francs mixed with coin that he had taken with him from the hotel, and inverting his pocket as he did it. He did not think that there was more than one hundred francs—twenty dollars—in all—extended in his open palm. "This is all I have," he said nervously.

"It will have to do," she said. She grabbed the cash, threw the envelope at Pine, and dashed out of the room, dropping the gun near the door as she left.

Pine retrieved the weapon and the envelope. The gun, although realistic, was a toy, stamped *fabriqué en Japon*; the envelope contained a single typewritten sheet, written in plain, clear English, and if it was true, it was worth, Pine reflected, a hell of a lot more than the thousand dollars that the Deplint woman had demanded of him. Pine was also sure that whoever had originally got the intelligence had been paid substantially more than the five thousand that had been paid to Pine.

Standing in the middle of the little room, Pine reread the page. It contained a list of Soviet missile sites in North Vietnam. Each site had been listed with a catalogue of its specific weaponry, and notations on the sheet indicated that all of the missiles at the several installations were fitted with fully armed, completely operative nuclear warheads.

Realizing the importance of the document, Pine decided to rid himself of the onerous paper as quickly as possible. He was not sure what action Washington would take when they had the information, but he was shocked that such weapons would be available in a volatile, war-torn area such as Nam.

As he got to the head of the stairs, however, he saw the body of Deplint's sister, lying on the landing below. Her throat had been severed from one end to the other, and blood had soaked the entire wooden floor upon which she lay. Kneeling over the body were two men, one of whom was going through the contents of her handbag, the other rifling through her clothing. A third man seemed to be hidden by the shadow of the banister.

27

"*Gar nichts!*" the man with the handbag said.

"*Auch nichts hier,*" the other replied. "*Vielleicht in dem Zimmer hinab?*"

The third man, who had a handkerchief to his nose, stepped out of the shadow and motioned with the white cloth.

"Stop that filthy muttering. You know I can't understand a word of German. What have you found?" There was no mistaking the high voice nor the American accent.

"Ve haf found nozzing, Herr Bikker,"replied one of the men. Moving into the light, his large waistline clearly visible now, Charles Bigger bent over the prone body. He was obviously repulsed by the goriness.

Pine stood at the top of the landing, holding his breath. Slowly, he started to back away, hoping to find another route out of the building.

He quietly crept up the few steps that he had taken on the stairway, and reentered the room he had just left. Going to the window, he checked the distance to the first landing, and judged it to be two flights; too far to jump. Since there were no fire escapes, and jumping did not seem provident, the only other alternative was to hide in another room, but he could hear Bigger and his killers at the top of the stairs, probably coming to recheck the room from which the woman had come. Through wavery glass, Pine could see an open window next door that beckoned invitingly. Stepping out onto the four-inch wide ledge, his heart jumping into his left ear, Pine made a wild and noisy scramble for the window of the room next door. His fingers just barely gripped the upper part of the casement and there he swung, back and forth, and with each swing, the window parted a little further from its hinge. Whipping his legs hard towards the building wall in an attempt to close the window, he tried to grab the inside of the frame with his left hand, his right still tightly gripping the top of the casement, which by now had begun to move in an arc away from the wall and from safety. His fingers were beginning to feel numb and the window was beginning to make the most horrendous sound.

Pine was positive that he would be heard at any moment and that if Bigger did spot him, he would suffer the same surgery as Deplint and his sister. Out of nowhere, it seemed, a sleepy female voice spoke to him in English.

"I had heard that France was a passionate country, but this is ridiculous."

A sleepy head poked aside the single curtain, and there stood the woman who had sat next to him on the airplane that morning.

"Well, don't just stand there," Pine said. "Haven't you ever seen a man hanging from a window before?" The woman, despite her consternation, had to smile.

"Why, you're, er, Mister—the guy from the plane today," she blurted as she got a look at him, and made a dash to the window to try to help.

"Here," hushed Pine. "Pull the window in towards you so I can jump in."

Grabbing the window's knob, she pulled Pine in towards her, and in a somewhat awkward manner he managed to scramble into the room, bruising his right hand, his elbow, his knee, and his pride.

"I must say, it's rather flattering that you thought enough to pay me such an odd visit, especially after the way you ignored me on the plane coming over," she grinned.

"Listen carefully," Pine whispered. "I'm in terrible trouble. You've got to help me. There are three men in the hall who will kill me if they can find me. Now, I know this sounds ridiculous, but you've got to believe me." He almost did not believe it himself.

"Say," she said. "You're not a spy or something, are you?"
Pine suppressed the biggest laugh he had felt in weeks. He

had the panicky feeling that he would never convince her in time.

"Look, just do me this one favor and hide me for a few minutes. Then later this evening, if you wish, as a token of appreciation, I'll take you to any place in Paris for dinner. I'll explain everything then. It's long and complicated, and I'm scared half to death right now and can't think too clearly and . . ." There was a knock at the door, and the handle was jiggled. The girl glanced around quickly in surprise.

"Get into my bed. Cover yourself up," she said. It was the only place in the room to hide.

Climbing into the bed, Pine felt as foolish and as naked as if he were nailed to the wall with the list pasted to his forehead.

Opening the door, the girl confronted Bigger's, "Sorry to intrude, Mademoiselle," enunciated in the worst French Pine had ever heard. She responded with a fluent barrage of probably the best French Pine had ever heard.

"Please, Miss, if you speak English. I've got to check your room. It is suspected that a thief is hiding in this building." The girl, responding in heavily accented English, continued the outrage.

"What do you mean? Who do you search? Me! I am no thief! I am here with my lover and you pound on the door. He push me out from the bed. Why you do this? Pierre, come to stop these men." She said the last to Pine, who was digging deeper into the mattress. He could not even think of an answer liquid enough to sound French. It was embarrassing that she could react so quickly, while he had to huddle in the sack, knowing that the men in the hall were killers. Pouncing on the first words that came to his mind, Pine uttered in the deepest and most Gallic sounding groan he could muster:

"Oh, *merde!*"

It was apparently enough, for after one look about from the door, Bigger and his friends excused themselves and left.

Springing from the bed, Pine pressed his ear to the thin door. In the hall, Bigger was instructing the others to wait in the lobby for an hour or so, to see if anyone came out. Although he did not expect that the American had come yet, they were to take no chances. It seemed that they had neither seen him nor heard him, and that they had merely checked the other rooms on that floor to be sure that no one else was there who was involved in the matter. On the way downstairs, Bigger told the others that if Pine were seen to arrive, they were not to molest him, but only to follow and keep track of him, until he made the pick-up. The rest of the instructions were lost as Bigger and the Germans descended to the next landing. Pine turned to a badly shaken young woman.

4

She was wearing nothing but a bathrobe. For some reason, without the mini-skirt, she seemed more helpless, despite her beautiful performance. Pine walked over to her and took her hands in his. Looking down into her deep brown eyes, which were now rimmed with tears, he felt a sense of protectiveness. It was rather ironic, since five minutes before, he lay cowering in her bed while she did the protecting.

"Look," he said softly. "It's all over now. You did fine."

She looked away from him and pulled her lips together, trying to recover her control, and Pine stepped to the window to give her a chance to collect herself. Although the room was slightly larger than number 33, it had approximately the same furnishings and interior design. There was also a dirty, oval throw rug on the floor.

"You know, I don't even know your name," Pine said in an attempt to break the tension.

With this confession, the girl began to sob anew, placing her face into her pillow. Pine dropped down next to her on the bed, and held her shoulders, feeling foolish. After a few minutes of soothing, she sat up, carefully wiping her eyes with the heels of her hands, to avoid smearing her make-up, although it was already merged into a single blot under each eye.

"Laura Kennedy," she said. "And for all I know, you *are* a thief. Who are you? Why did you come here? I don't know why I did what I did for you. Now maybe I'm in trouble with the police." She was trembling, and again her composure was beginning to slip.

"Now wait a minute," Pine said evenly. "I said I would explain, but you must give me some time. I have to get to the American Embassy as soon as I can get away from here. Then, as I promised, we can go to dinner, if you wish. At dinner I'll tell you what I can. By the way, that was a terrific performance you gave," he added with a smile.

Laura suppressed a grin through tearful eyes, then looked straight up at him. "Can't you tell me a little now? Something that will let me trust you even a little?" she pleaded.

Pine thought for a moment. How much could he tell her? He really did not even know who she was. He needed her help, but if he involved her, it would place her in danger as well. It would not be fair.

"You surely couldn't believe that I'm a thief. What could I be stealing in this miserable place? And besides, that guy at the door was as American as air conditioning; you didn't really think that he was with any French authority, did you? He couldn't even speak French properly. Look, those guys were killers, and they're after me because I know something that can hurt them. Now don't get excited, but they just killed a girl on the landing below, although I expect that by now they will have removed the body. I've got to get to the Embassy as soon as possible and they are going to try to stop me because what I am going to do is to put them out of business. Nothing must stop me—it's that important."

He could see that Laura was trying to believe his impossible story, and he figured that he had told her enough of the truth to get by for now.

"We'll have to wait a while until the men downstairs go away, so do you mind if I stay a little longer? We can talk."

"Well, I guess since you're here already, there's no reason why you shouldn't stay a bit. But I don't mind telling you that I don't like it." She rose and straightened her bathrobe, suddenly feeling self-conscious at the state of her undress. "You know," she said. "You haven't told me *your* name yet."

"Oh, sorry," he replied. "Pine. Mark Pine. I'm a lawyer. In New York," he added, as an afterthought.

"What are you doing in Paris?" she asked.

"It's a business trip. But what are you doing in this dump, might be more to the point."

"You mean, what's a nice girl like me doing in a place like this?" she said smiling. "Actually, my mother stayed here in this very room some thirty years ago, when she was a student in Paris. The Sorbonne is right down the street, you know. I thought it would be romantic to stay in the same place as she did. I made the reservations from New York; I hadn't seen it then. Tomorrow I'll try to find another room."

"I think that you'd better try to find one this afternoon. I can help you find a place when I finish with the Embassy, if you'd like.

"You know, as I think of it, it might not be such a bad idea if you left with me," Pine continued. "You can come to the Embassy, and from there, we can go room hunting. How long will you be staying in Paris?"

"About a month, I guess," she said. "It depends on how ideas go. I'm working on a novel. Say listen, if I'm going to leave with you, I'll have to get dressed or something."

"Or something," Pine said looking again at the bare legs that protruded from the slit in her bathrobe.

"You couldn't very well step outside for a moment, I suppose," she remarked. "Would you at least turn around, please?"

With his back turned, Pine could hear hasty rustling and sliding of clothing over what his imagination supposed was a firm soft body. It did not take her more than a minute or so to dress, and when he turned around, she was blushing slightly, which gave her eyes an even darker and more luxurious look. She was wearing a tweed skirt, ribbed sweater with long sleeves and plain round neck, and a pair of simple medium heel shoes. He could see that she was not more than about twenty-four or so, and apparently of comfortable means, if her clothing and luggage were any indication.

"Do you think we can leave yet?" she asked, noticing the manner in which he was appraising her.

"I think we'd better wait a while. I heard the fat man tell the others to wait an hour or so, to be sure that nobody left the building."

Since there were no chairs in the room, they sat on the bed. Pine told her about himself. He did not tell her the reason that he was in Paris, but suggested that a client had sent him to France for some business that he had already completed that morning. It sounded frail, even to him.

She explained that her father owned a flourishing chain of small department stores in the Midwest, and that she had moved to New York after college to write. She had already published two small novels, but explained that she was not proud of the style nor of the subject matter, and had hoped to make a breakthrough with her present book, so that she could use her own name, "without embarrassing the family," she said. On an impulse, Pine reached across, and rather clumsily, attempted to kiss her.

"Now wait a minute," she said hotly. "I don't know what you expected, but I don't have any intention of playing any of these games with you here like this. I guess I should mention that I have someone waiting for me in New York."

"Look, I'm sorry." Pine felt himself blushing, more from his awkwardness, than from what he had tried. "I mean, it was just . . . Oh, you know."

Fine spy he was, he thought. Female number one robs him; female number two rebuffs him. He began to feel that the job was not worth the effort, if he could not have the fringe benefits as well.

"Don't be embarrassed," Laura said more calmly. "I guess it was partly my fault anyway."

Pine checked his watch. It was ten after twelve. Opening the door slowly, he checked to see if anyone was on the landing. He motioned Laura to stay behind him, and after looking carefully, he stepped back into the room.

"Be as quiet as you can. Take your shoes off. Now follow me down the stairs a few paces behind, and if anything goes wrong, just try to get to the Embassy. Tell them that I sent you. Someone there will help you, I guess. Are you ready?"

Laura nodded uncomfortably, and they picked their way out of the room. Pine stopped suddenly and motioned her back inside.

"Listen, you'd better pack now and bring your stuff with you. It might not be safe to come back here later."

Without a word, she went over to her two open suitcases, threw a few things into one of them, and closed the latches.

"I didn't get much of a chance to unpack. I knew I wouldn't be staying here more than one night after I saw the place. And besides . . ."

"How about us getting out of here?" Pine interrupted politely.

Laura smiled and they started again towards the stairway, Pine carrying the larger of the two cases. It was remarkable how heavy it was. With each careful step on the stairs, Pine could feel his hackles bristling. Every creak sounded as loud as a siren, but he realized that the noise would be less noticeable to one who had been listening to the old building for an hour. What was he going to do if the two Germans were still at the bottom of the stairs?

When they got to the next landing, Laura saw the blood stains, although Bigger and his associates had removed the body. He could see that she was beginning to believe his story from her expression of surprise and horror. They continued to descend, and when they reached the last landing, Pine motioned her to wait there until he had indicated that it was safe to follow. Putting the suitcase on the top step, he softly sidled down, step by step, trying to keep his weight as close to the wall as possible, to avoid any extra loud creaks. The closer he got to the bottom, the surer he was that no one was there. On the last step, he began to feel foolish again. Walking gingerly to the large double door, leading to the street, he eased one side open and peeked outside.

The thing that hit him on the shoulder, must have missed his head by a hair's breadth. As it was, he almost fainted from the pain. Reflex, however, is a remarkable thing, and despite the pain and fear, his Marine experience came rushing back to him, a bit rusty, perhaps, but basically intact.

Almost as soon as the blow had landed on Pine's left shoulder, his right foot shot back in a traditional karate kick that was part of the Marine training he had received almost nine years before. The groan his assailant uttered was accompanied by a loud crash as his victim fell over backwards onto the banister. Before Pine had a chance to turn to see him, the other German was upon him with a large, ugly looking knife held in a manner that suggested that he knew how to use it. Circling slowly, Pine affected the long disused crouch, and waited for his opportunity to close. Watching only the eyes of the man in front of him, he snapped back into the old habits and confidence flooded back into his system with a force that surprised him almost as much as it pleased him.

Although the man with the knife was perhaps in his late fifties, he seemed in top shape. Pine hoped the German's age would slow his reflexes sufficiently to give Pine some help, which, God knew, he needed. The German suddenly shot forward with surprising speed and the blade cut through Pine's jacket sleeve, digging shallowly into the flesh. The pain heightened Pine's attention. Reaching out for the man's knife arm, Pine shot a quick glancing blow off the German's forearm and countered with a straight jab to the midsection. The blow did some damage. The German doubled over slightly and Pine, seizing the opportunity and the offensive, grabbed the wrist of the German's knife hand and brought the rigid side of his flat open palm sharply into the center of his opponent's Adam's apple. There was a loud cracking sound. The German dropped the knife and stood looking agape, his eyes wide open, his lips trying to make a word. Slowly his face contorted and flushed as he sank to his knees. Pine watched the slow process of asphyxiation in fascination, willing the man to die. Finally the German just lay there, not moving, eyes wide open, his hands at his throat, his face stretched in a pitiful grimace. In horror, Pine realized that he was dead.

Remembering the other German, from whom he had heard nothing during the ninety seconds or so that the fight with the other had taken, Pine turned. He was standing in an odd position with his head against the banister. His eyes too were wide open. There was no expression on his face, and blood dripped out of one ear. Laura was standing at the top of the landing, leaning over and watching with terror in her face. She finally said:

"His head, his head! On the banister, look."

Pine looked carefully at the German who lay against the banister. Projecting from the old decaying woodwork was a rusty spike, against which he had fallen after being kicked by Pine. The spike had impaled the back of his head and it was this that caused the German to remain in his somewhat upright position against the banister. It was also the cause of his death.

Pine turned to the back of the hallway and was sick for a few minutes. Turning, he saw Laura standing there with large wet eyes. She came over and wiped his face with her handkerchief.

"I saw. They tried to kill you. You were marvelous. But it's so horrible." She did not know what to say anymore than did Pine in the face of such sudden violence.

Gathering his courage, Pine returned to the two bodies. With disgust, he searched each methodically, holding his breath, for he imagined that he could smell the death upon them. Neither man had a single item of identification on his person. One of them had a package of cheap cigarettes and a Zippo lighter; the other had nothing. Pulling the first German off the banister, Pine dragged and shuffled him and then the other into a corner of the hall behind the staircase. Then he was sick again. Returning to the landing to retrieve Laura's case, he and the girl stepped out into the bright sunlight.

5

Despite the sun and the brisk autumn weather, Pine felt as though he were suffocating. In addition, his left arm was beginning to throb more noticeably and blood was seeping through the sleeve of the torn jacket. Pulling up the jacket sleeve and that of the shirt beneath it for inspection, he saw that the German's razor sharp knife had make a clean slash about three-and-a-half inches long, but not particularly deep. He led Laura around the corner to his hotel and escorted her upstairs under the approving eye of the clerk. The ratty little bellhop raised an eyebrow, obviously impressed by the speed with which Pine had apparently worked. Pine almost wished that the little bastard would say something so that he would have an excuse to reshape his nose.

Back in his room, he washed, allowed Laura to administer to his wound, changed his shirt and suit and finally placed a call through to the Embassy. He was not sure exactly whom he should speak to, so he asked for the Chief Security Officer whose secretary took the call.

"Why yes, Mr. Pine," she purred primly. "We've been expecting a call from you."

"I can't talk now. Is your boss in?"

"He just stepped out for a moment. Would you like to hold?"

"No. Just tell him that I'm coming down immediately. Something got pretty badly screwed up." "Screwed up" got precisely the reaction he had hoped it would.

Pine turned to Laura.

"I don't think that it would be a good idea for you to come with me."

"If you think I'm staying here . . ."

"Now don't start playing games with me, Laura." Pine glanced out the window. Everything seemed quiet; at least he had not yet heard police klaxons. "I'm only going to be gone for about half an hour. You get some rest, now. I awakened you anyway when I barged in. When I get back, I'll waken you, don't worry."

Before she could reply, Pine strode out of the room. Upon reaching the street, he flagged down a cab and asked to be taken to the American Embassy. The driver shrugged as if to suggest that only an idiot would go to such a place when so many other more interesting sites were available, but floored the accelerator anyway. It seemed that he kept it floored all the way to Place de la Concorde where the heavily crowded Right Bank traffic compelled him once again to show respect for life and limb.

Tossing a five franc note to the driver, which was much in excess of the fare, Pine paced quickly towards the entrance of the Embassy without waiting for change. The driver de-cabbed, stood on the running board, and shouted, waving the fiver over his head:

"*Merci, Monsieur, merci. Vous voudriez que je garde votre*

41

place? Alors, Monsieur . . . hein, les Americains sont fou."
Pretending that he did not know the cab driver, Pine walked into the reception area of the Embassy.

"I have an appointment with your Chief Security Officer. My name is Pine," he said, feeling self-conscious.

"Won't you have a seat, sir. I'll let him know you're here."
The young woman behind the desk buzzed a number on the switchboard and spoke quietly into the mouthpiece of a chest phone, looked up and smiled at Pine. Shortly, a very tall and very ugly woman of indeterminate age waddled over to him, smiled, and asked him to follow her. Pine smiled back, not out of friendliness, but in self-defense; three words and he knew the purr of the C.S.O.'s secretary, and prim she wasn't.

They walked down a long corridor and after traversing what seemed like a maze, they arrived in front of an ornate old door that contained a black panel firmly bolted to its center. It said "Private." His escort knocked twice and opened the door inwards, standing to the side so Pine could enter.

"Come in Mr. Pine. It's good to see you again."

"Why Mr. Bigger. It's good to see you again, too." Pine almost choked on the words and did not wait to be asked to sit. Rather he collapsed into a deep chair. He should have expected it, he reflected. After all, nothing had gone wrong for at least twenty minutes.

"You seem to be distressed, Mr. Pine." Bigger was acting rather guardedly and his little pig eyes had not left Pine's face for an instant.

Pine realized that, so far, Bigger had not said nor done anything to indicate that he knew Pine had seen him at the drop site. He also realized that his story had better be convincing; the fat man could have him stashed somewhere from which all his ravings about Bigger would not extricate him.

"Well, you're damn right I'm upset. First of all you give me this dance around about picking up a package. You tell me that there's no danger, although I should have suspected something when you paid me five grand. But when I get there, not only is the place empty, but it looks like it's been that way for ages. I figure that whoever is coming will be back, so I leave and plan on returning from time to time." Pine could feel his bladder rapidly approaching the burst point.

He knew that Bigger's agents would have called him had anyone arrived, and he knew that they were in no condition to make calls to anyone, so he had to account for their absence and for the missing call.

"You also told me that there would be no rough stuff," he said accusingly. "Well, let me tell you buddy boy, you'll never pull that song and dance on me again."

Bigger looked ready to pounce, eyes slitted, huge jowls quivering, as tense as a cuckold caught in a closet. And all Pine could concentrate on was his passionate urge to relieve himself.

"When I get back downstairs after finding nobody home," he continued, "I notice that there's blood on the ground floor landing. So naturally, I look around. And in the back of the staircase, there were two men, both dead, with blood all over the floor and everything. I don't know what's going on, but I . . ."

Bigger had risen from his seat and with a wild look in his eyes rushed over to Pine with that incredible lightness of foot that fat men at times possess. Had he touched him, Pine would have wet his pants.

"They were dead? Both were dead?" Bigger blurted. "When was this? Do you know what time it was?" Still obviously upset and as an afterthought, he asked, "Was there any message for us in the room?"

"No. There was nothing at all in the room," Pine replied. "And it was no more than thirty minutes ago."

Bigger walked slowly to the window and looked out over

Paris' streets. Bringing his hand up to his forehead, he wiped away a row of sweat beads and began to crack his knuckles. Finally he turned around.

"I'm sorry, Mr. Pine. You have no idea how sorry I am. It looks as if you have done your job well, under the circumstances. There is really nothing else that you can do now."

"Does that mean that I can leave Paris? What about the money you gave me?" Pine realized that he had to get away from Bigger and turn the intelligence over to some proper authority. At present, stuck in his inside jacket pocket, it was giving him heartburn.

"Yes you can go and the money is yours. Well . . . actually, it might be better if you stayed in Paris for another day or so. Perhaps I can find out if that information can be obtained through another source, and then we may need you. Where are you staying? Oh, yes. The Candide."

Pine suddenly felt that his arm had started to bleed again. He could feel the wetness on the bottom of the bandages. That was all he needed, for the blood to seep through the jacket now. Bigger would then know everything. And damn it, it was also the only suit he had left with him in Paris, and the good one at that. Bigger was speaking again.

"Did you report the dead men to the police?"

"No. I thought that perhaps you should know first," he lied.

"Then if you wanted to make a report, you could do it yourself. I don't know what's going on and I don't want to know what's going on. I just want to get out of here."

"Well, you can go home now, Mr. Pine. That is, back to your hotel. We'll contact you there later today if we need you again. At any rate, call us tomorrow afternoon and if there is nothing by then, you can return to New York if you like." Pine knew that Bigger would not contact him.

Bigger was sweating profusely by now, although the room was quite cool. Pine was too, and besides his now almost desperate need to urinate, his arm felt as if there were enough blood swishing around in the soggy bandages to float the Spanish Armada.

"I'll call you tomorrow, then, Mr. Bigger," Pine said as he rose to leave, surreptitiously checking the chair's cloth arm for blood stains. Happily, there were none.

Despite his need of a bathroom, Pine was more eager to get out of the Embassy. Walking stiffly from the building, he saw that his friendly cabbie had got into an argument with another driver, and was still there. His final lurid description of the other driver's mixed ancestry and cultural heritage would have done justice to the most studied bigot. Upon seeing him, the cabbie gave the other driver the French equivalent of the high sign, and rushed over to Pine to escort him to the cab. On the return ride, he did not stop telling Pine how wonderful Americans were. Pine concentrated only upon controlling the desperate urge in his groin.

At the hotel, Pine gave the driver exactly what was on the meter and no tip. Turning out of curiosity as he dashed into the building, he saw the driver standing beside his cab, holding out the palm of his hand with a vacant incomprehensible gaze.

Laura was fast asleep in bed. She had taken off all her clothing and placed it in a neat pile on the low dresser. He slipped quietly and quickly into the bathroom. Returning to retrieve his first aid kit after a few moments, he relocked himself in the bathroom, and removed his jacket and shirt, neither of which had yet become soiled with blood. Despite the sensation that it had been soaked, the blood had not yet come through, and Pine left the bathroom, relieved.

Pine flopped into the only comfortable chair in the room and attempted to think. The delivery of the list of weapons was his first priority. He did not know what Washington could do about it, but realized that the more time they had the better. The main problem was to convey the information to somebody trustworthy in the government. But Bigger had told him not to leave Paris that day. If he did, Bigger would get suspicious, and then Pine would find himself either dead, or sufficiently involved in self-protective activities, that he would be unable to devote time to getting rid of the intelligence. Since he had the list himself, he knew that Bigger's further searches could yield nothing. He would be able to depart the next day, and hard as it would be, he would have to wait.

He was also worried about Laura. If he told her too much, it might increase her danger. It was still only two o'clock and that would give him time to get her a place to stay, take her to dinner, and kiss her good-bye, if she would let him.

Feeling better because he now knew his course of action, or rather inaction, Pine rested his head back to try to get a few minutes sleep. As he did so, however, Laura sat up, holding the blanket in front of her.

"Oh, you're back." Intuitively obvious to the most casual observer. "Why didn't you get me up?"

"I was fearful that in shock and excitement at finding a strange man in your bedroom, you would jump out of bed and attack. This time you're even less decently dressed and I thought that the strain would be too much for me." Pine said with an elegant flourish.

"Oh, cut it out."

"Come on. Get dressed so we can find a place for you to stay."

She looked at him for a moment without speaking and glanced down at the large french bed. Blushing, she leaped out, carrying the blankets with her, and walked to the bathroom taking her clothes with her.

"What happened at the Embassy?" she called over the rush of water.

"I'll tell you about it at dinner. First, let's get you set for the night."

In a shorter time than he had expected, she emerged. Pine was impressed by how attractive she looked in the fresh clothing she had selected. Leaving her bags behind and leading her by the arm, Pine guided Laura out into the cool air of what had suddenly promised to become a much more pleasant day than at first it appeared.

The clerks at the various decent hotels they tried looked at Pine and Laura strangely and muttered their various versions of "no vacancy" with varying degrees of impudence. On a sudden impulse, Pine dragged Laura back to his own hotel, and asked the clerk if he could find a room for the lady. The clerk shrugged his shoulders in a fashion that meant everything from apples to pomegranates, looked at Pine as if he were an Italian *castrato*, and crazy to boot, and flipped another key to him.

After installing Laura in her room, Pine returned to his to get some rest. Laura had insisted that he do this when she was certain that he would tell her nothing until dinner; besides, she explained, she had things to do. Women always had "things to do"; it scared him. Returning to his room, Pine called the clerk and told him to ring him at six-thirty; he fell quickly to sleep. His dreams were wonderfully indecent.

6

Charles Bigger had always had two ambitions in life. He wanted to be tall and slim and he wanted to be important. Nature had foiled him in one respect and he had foiled himself in the other. Physically, Bigger was an impressively repulsive man. He was short, fat, and bald and it seemed that with each passing year, he became shorter, fatter, and balder. But his great circumference was not the reason for his unique unpleasantness. Perhaps, as a result of his physical conformation, perhaps because of his childhood, he had become a man of excessive tastes, excessive vices, and excessive ambitions.

From early childhood, Bigger had been deprived of almost every luxury afforded a normal child, even one from mean origins. His father had met his mother briefly, but sufficiently, resulting in an unwanted birth that developed into a strong dislike for the child by the time he was five. If not for this reason alone, then for related causes, Bigger did not become fully toilet trained until he was about seven years of age. Rumor of this had got to his friends, or rather acquaintances, since he did not easily mix with people even as a child, adding to the stresses of growing up. His mother, who supplemented her waitress's income in a manner that derived its origins from ancient times, tended to expend her bounty on her more necessary staples, such as cheap booze and make-up, leaving little, if any, for the support of the evidence of her earlier indiscretion.

In 1926, at the age of ten, Charles Bigger left the seamier side of New York and set out on his own to wend his way through the devious paths of life. His mother spent one entire evening crying on the breast of an understanding client and succeeded in obtaining a bonus for her sorrows. The bonus was considerably more attractive than Bigger and induced a new bedtime pitch that somewhat increased her standard of living.

Needless to say, life was neither pleasant nor prosperous for the ten-year-old vagrant, but by one means or another, he reached the age of seventeen, whereupon he personally discovered for the first time that women were good for something other than an occasional free meal. Although he found his initial experiences interesting, he soon learned that his true interests lay with members of his own sex, and that women, gainfully employed in a proper manner, could provide the wherewithal to obtain greater enjoyment and luxury. By nineteen, Bigger had one of the largest stables in Chicago.

At about this time, he was approached by representatives of several organized syndicates who indicated that they would be appreciative if he would either consent to terminate his activities in Chicago, or to terminate his ambition of attaining lawful age. Having got used to the luxury that accompanies large incomes, Bigger had developed a passionate love of life,

49

and his courage, which had never been one of his excesses, did not extend to things physical. Packing a hasty bag, Bigger returned to New York City accompanied by something in the area of one hundred thousand dollars in medium-sized bills, and an unusually complete education in subjects generally overlooked in conventional schools.

One of the things that had always impressed Charles Bigger was clothing. He fully believed that clothes made the man, and proceeded to collect large quantities of beautifully hand-made clothing as soon as he was able to afford the expense that his hard-to-fit shape dictated. His diet, which had become well-known to most restauranteurs in Chicago by 1936, consisted of anything served in large quantities, especially if it was expensive. Upon his return to New York, he never gave up the habit of expensive dress, no matter how much deprivation in other areas it required; but his diet suffered continually.

It did not take long for Bigger to discover that the New York mobs were as unwilling to admit newcomers into competition as were those in Chicago, and through the middle of 1939, Bigger was reduced to smaller industries on the outskirts of the principal vice routes. Notwithstanding his involvement in the many areas of petty crime, or perhaps because it was so petty, he did manage to keep his name out of police files and the like, a task that was easier in the days of the rackets, especially as he was, until 1937, a minor and beneath the notice of the established law enforcement agencies.

After Pearl Harbor, although his size kept him out of the service, Bigger took a job as a minor police guard in one of the foreign services of the United States. His apparently clean record and his familiarity with police methods, learned the hard way, qualified him for the position that he felt might offer some opportunity for ill-gotten gains. There he had his first taste of true elegance and saw without question, what that elusive term "class" truly meant. At parties and receptions that were held for various personages, he, as a blank-faced guard, was able to observe the manners and the etiquette of the so-called polite society; and thus the facade for his future life had its inception.

Realizing that one need not have money to live well if he followed a profession that lived well, he decided to make his career in the foreign service. To give credit where due, it may be said that he quite positively put aside his baser instincts in the pursuit of his new image.

During the war years, and for a period thereafter, Bigger kept track of all the people who had known him in his prior life, and marked off names as each either died, was eliminated or in some cases, was executed. By 1947, Bigger had succeeded in gaining a reputation as a clever operator, having employed his underworld knowledge to entrap or otherwise capture government offenders whose cases had been assigned to him for investigation. More important assignments began to shift to his small office, and by this time too, only three of Bigger's former acquaintances, who could still pull the plug on his warm bath, remained alive. With deft cunning, employing his newfound powers, he succeeded in having all three transported to a more peaceful and permanent world.

Now, for the first time, Bigger felt free to expand his activities in his department. His rise to position was both rapid and surprisingly justified. He was a good government agent.

Then, one day late in 1952, he was approached by representatives of an organization that confronted him with a record of all his prior misdeeds, including photographs of his perversions. They indicated that the lot could be purchased in exchange for a small favor of political nature. The information they sought was not particularly hard for Bigger to acquire and, in fact, was not even of importance; but after having performed this one small task for his persecutors, their hold was even more tenacious. From then on, he was required to provide more and more information and to perform bigger and better subversions in their behalf. The dossier they had finally collected on him, together with his actions in subversion of his government, was sufficient to lock him into their organization for life; that they paid him well for his services was enough to assuage his inconstant conscience.

On this particular fall evening, Bigger found himself walking quickly along a secluded section of the Quai along the Left Bank of the Seine. Across the river he could see the modern outline of the television transmission building and the vapor from his short quick breaths caused him to envy the interior warmth of that white edifice. A short distance down the street he saw a dark Citroën parked with its motor running.

"Boris?" he said as he peered into the car from the passenger side.

"Shut up, you fool." Boris did not seem particularly happy. "Why have you called me?"

"What do you want from me?" Bigger's whine was defensive. "Something unexpected has come up."

"Do you not know that it is dangerous for us to meet at this time? If you can not do what you are told, and do it effectively, we will have no further use for you." Bigger had got into the back seat and was rubbing his hands briskly together.

"The information that we tried to intercept has become misplaced." Bigger said it simply and quickly.

"You imbecile! You know how important that list is to my people. It must be retrieved."

"But we tried, comrade," Bigger pleaded. "In fact, at first I suspected the American, but he is, I am sure, innocent. He seems to be too frightened by what has happened and I do not think he has the art to deceive me."

"Don't give me your opinions, you pig. Tell me what has

happened, every detail of it. I will decide; I will opine."

Bigger related the events of the past few days to Boris, starting from the first meeting with Diver at Pine's office in New York. When he had finished, the Slav just sat there quietly playing with a bit of rubber moulding hanging from the window frame of the car. When he finally spoke, his voice was surprisingly quiet and collected.

"It is this Pine, I am sure," he said. "We know that the information was reduced to a writing. We know that Deplint's sister had the list. When you found her, there was nothing on her person. Hence she must have either placed it somewhere for safe keeping or given it to the American, since she knew that he was to get it. What else could she be doing in that building if not to meet Pine? He must have got to her before you did." The Slav turned to Bigger.

"You must have him searched, and his room. Do not kill him unless it is absolutely necessary. There have been too many killings already, and with each one, the chances of a mistake being made increases. Do you understand?" The Slav looked pointedly at Bigger. "After you have the list, we will take care of this Pine."

Bigger nodded his assent.

"Don't worry. I will take care of it."

"When someone tells 'do not worry,' I start to worry," Boris remarked. "Be sure that there are no mistakes this time or you are a dead man." Bigger believed him without the slightest doubt.

The Citroën pulled away quickly leaving Bigger the walk back to the main stream of traffic, where he hoped to get a cab. The idea that Pine had pulled a fast one on him injured his already dented ego. That sonofabitch, he thought. I'll break his balls for this.

Rushing back to his apartment to plan the night's activities, he reflected how lucky it was that the permanent Chief of

Security at the Embassy was in Washington, taking a long overdue leave, so that he, as second-in-command, could have free access to the files and equipment that he would need. His regular position in Investigations would never have enabled him to accomplish what had to be done as quickly as he had to do it. En route to his apartment, Bigger stopped to phone three men and instructed them to meet him there. When he arrived, two of them had preceded him; the third came shortly thereafter. Pine would get his!

Pine awakened after about an hour. He felt refreshed, and although his shoulder was badly bruised and beginning to stiffen, and the wound on his left arm was redly inflamed, he had a certain light-hearted attitude about it all. Perhaps it was Laura or perhaps it was the relief of having got out of the day's activities in one piece, more or less. Tomorrow, he reflected, he should get clearance to go home; surely, Bigger could not suspect him of any subterfuge. It was seven o'clock, and Laura was putting on the last touches when he arrived at her door.

"Come on in and make yourself comfortable, Mark," she called, in answer to his knock. "I'll be done in a minute."

"Don't rush," he replied, stretching out on her bed with his hands behind his head. The motion wreaked momentary havoc on his shoulder, but the pressure against the cut on his forearm eased its throbbing as pressure on a sore tooth can relieve its pain.

"Listen," she scolded from another side of the room, "don't you think for one moment that I'm going to let you take me out of here until you tell me more of what's going on."

"That's fine with me," Pine smiled. "We can stay here for ... well ... I guess that I could last about a month, if you let me rest every few hours or so."

Laura stepped into the center of the room. Wearing a simple black dress that began slightly lower than it should have and ended slightly higher than it should have, she was beyond a man's fondest fantasies. Her hair, which she had been wearing pulled back, was now piled on top of her head, revealing a long expanse of neck that made the dress seem lower cut than it was. A single strand of pearls draped about her neck. Her stockings were flesh colored, and black high heels accented her long graceful legs. At that moment, Pine felt that he was in love with her; at least one part of him was sure of it.

Noticing his grimace of pain as he attempted to sit upright, she walked over to him and placed her hands gently on his shoulders.

"Does it bother you very much?" she inquired. "Perhaps you should see a doctor?"

"No. Not really," he said. "I'll be all right in a few days. It's only a bruise; nothing broken."

"Would you like me to rub it for you? You could tell me about what's happening while I did it."

"Well, okay." He began to remove his jacket, then his tie and shirt. "A client of mine in the clothing business was missing shipments from Hong Kong. While I was looking into it for him, I uncovered something that led me to believe that the shipments had been misrouted to Paris." It was getting more difficult to speak over the pleasure of having his back massaged. The waves of relaxation were overwhelming.

"As soon as I got here though—a little lower and towards the center please—I discovered something more sinister," he fabricated. "It appeared that narcotics were being stuffed into the hems of the garments and whole shipments were being smuggled into the United States at different entry points. I was about to notify the Embassy, but before I could do anything, the smugglers got on to me." Pine stopped to see how she was taking it. She seemed totally noncommittal.

"At any rate, I didn't get the full story until I got up to that

55

horrid hotel room next door to yours. It was apparently a drop of some kind where some of the goods had been hidden. They came back and that's where you came in."

"What about that murdered girl you told me about?"

"Well, she was the one who led me to them. They got to her as she was leaving; it's what warned me when I heard the noise."

Laura looked skeptically at Pine and thought for a moment. Digging her fingers deeply into his back she extricated a sharp groan from him.

"If that's what you're going to tell me, I guess I'll have to go along with it, for a while. But don't think you're going to get away with that one for long."

Laura stood up and straightened her dress front. She walked to the mirror and patty-caked her hair a few times, then turned to face Pine.

"You're a terrible liar, Pine old buddy, but because I'm getting hungry, I'll accept your story for now. Are you hungry yet?"

"I get hungrier every minute," he said looking directly into her eyes with the beginnings of a smile on his lips. "Come here a minute," he said softly.

Hesitating a moment, she finally walked over to his side. Pulling her down to him, he pressed her body against his naked breast and kissed her gently and tenderly. She resisted for a moment, almost long enough to be convincing and then slowly yielded fully to his caress and to his lips. And as he kissed her his hand slowly moved down the side of her face, onto her shoulder and softly down her side, his thumb running lightly over her breast. Her body seemed to flow with his hand and she drifted into his mood.

Laura sat up suddenly. Her face was flushed. Her breath was short. She swallowed and pressed her lips together, the tip of her tongue jetting out to wet the center of her upper lip. She closed her eyes slowly.

"I think we'd better get out of here," she said. "I wish I didn't like you, you know." She spoke gently; he could still taste her.

Except for a few idlers, the lobby was empty as they passed through to the street. A cab pulled up and the couple stepped in. Pine bent over towards the driver for a moment and the cab sped away towards its destination. As it turned the corner, a black Peugeot pulled away from the opposite curb and began to follow the cab at a discreet distance.

7

The clerk at the Candide Hotel stood behind the reception desk, finishing the last details of his job for the night. After completing the registration cards for the new guests that had arrived that day, they would be sent to the police Registrar and he could return to his crossword puzzle. The dark man who leaned against the wall opposite his reception desk reading a paper disinterestedly, looked up every time a guest walked out towards the door. The clerk did not like it when the police came to his hotel while he was on duty because it always meant extra work for him. It was bad enough that French Law required all foreigners to be registered with the police when they checked into a hotel, but when the police came to check up on one of them, it could mean trouble. And trouble meant even more work.

This time, as the dark man looked up at the clerk, the clerk nodded his head slightly and looked back at him. The strange American and his Miss Kennedy were just about leaving. The dark man spoke softly over his lapel. Only three people heard his words. One was standing outside opposite the hotel; one was in a cab, dressed as a driver; one was in a black Peugeot parked down the street.

As Pine and Laura stepped into the street, the cab pulled up alongside the couple. After the cab had pulled away, the man standing opposite the hotel walked slowly across the street and entered the Candide. He approached the dark man and the two of them went to the elevator and on to Pine's room.

Jacques Pomey had been with the *Deuxième Bureau* for almost twenty years. He was used to being disturbed at odd hours of the night by his superiors. This time, however, he had been surprised by the call he had got, just as he had started dinner. Friday nights were usually quiet in his department, unless he was assigned to a case. On this evening, his boss had called and asked him to return to the Bureau at once. Arriving some twenty minutes later, he met dark, little Cambert who apparently had also been summoned by the Chief. Inside the shabby little office were the Chief, Dubois, and Packer. Pomey hoped that he would not have to work with Packer, who was a Jew. Pomey hated Jews; he also hated people who wore modern clothing, who drank alcoholic beverages (other than wine) or who were intolerant; he was a moderate man.

The Chief explained that information was about that an American possessed a document of value to the French Republic, and that an American Embassy defector, working with the Russians, was to search the American's room that night while he slept. It was the Chief's idea to search the room before the Soviet organization could do so. He instructed Cambert to wait inside the hotel and to get the desk clerk to identify the American if he came down. Packer was to wait on foot across the street from the hotel so that he could follow if the American decided to walk. Dubois was to get a cab and wait by the hotel in case the American decided to ride. Pomey was to wait with a driver in a Bureau vehicle so he could follow the cab or Packer, depending on who was tail. If the American left for the evening, the two unused "hounds" were to search his room while he was out. If he did not go out by ten, he was to be arrested, brought to the Bureau, after which the Chief would profusely apologize for the identity error. In any event the room was to be searched. The American was to followed, but not molested.

Pomey had his driver follow the cab past Odéon and into the Boulevard St. Germaine. On the Boule, the cab turned right, then left again towards the Quai and the Seine. Pomey followed the cab across the river into the Place de la Concorde, up the Champs and into Avenue Marbeuf, where the cab stopped in front of an expensive restaurant. Pine and the girl got out, Pine handing some cash over the top of the seat to the driver, and entered the crowded restaurant.

The bar on the right was packed with milling shapes. Although there were many people in the room, the noise level was low and Pine, who had made a reservation before his afternoon nap, accosted the harried *Maitre d'Hote*, who apologized that there would be a few minutes wait until the table was free. He and the girl fought their way into the crush at the bar and by the time he had placed his order, a Cinzano for Laura and a Dewer's whiskey with a dab of water for himself, the table was ready; the drinks were brought to table by the *Maitre d'Hote*.

They were given seats against the front wall in an intimate

enclosure. Around the walls of the room were large glass cases in which sides of beef were hung on hooks. The restaurant had the good smell of many beef dishes cooked in different sauces.

"This is a lovely place," Laura commented, looking around at the other diners who were eating in the casual and unhurried manner that is custom in France.

"It used to be one of my favorites, a few years ago." Pine thought momentarily of his wealthy widow, Pam, and of the times they had eaten here together. In fact, it was one of the few really good restaurants in Paris that he knew where an order of beef would not disappoint an American who needed more than a thin sliver to sate his urge.

The waiter took their order for hors d'oeuvres, Beluga caviar with toast ends, and returned in a few moments with a large bowl of shiny black fish eggs and a basket of French bread that had been lightly heated, the French equivalent of toast. As they ate and spoke of light matters, Pine occasionally reflected inwardly that he should have left the letter back at the hotel. It was too dangerous to walk around with in his pocket, but he did not want it out of his sight for fear it would disappear. Laura was radiant and seemed to be enjoying herself. She kept looking up at Pine and smiling; she was consuming large quantities of caviar on small torn-off bits of bread.

"Hey, listen," Pine smiled. "There's more to this dinner on the way. Don't fill yourself up on baby cannon balls."

"Don't worry," she said over her drink. "I didn't get a chance to eat this afternoon and I'm ready to eat that whole side of beef on the wall over there, glass case and all."

The caviar was superb and shortly after they had finished the last remains, the waiter returned to remove the bowl and the uneaten bread. The captain then came over to take the dinner order.

Pine, after briefly consulting the menu, placed it on the side of the table.

"Let me order for you, Laura." She was agreeable.

"I think we shall begin with baked langoustine, stuffed with crab meat, à la cointreau. Then the *vichyssoise*, the chateaubriand for two, no sauces with that, please, candied carrots, *pommes-frites*. After that a mixed salad, cheese dressing. We'll place the rest of the order later. Could you send over the wine steward?" Pine looked up at Laura who was peering at him speculatively.

The wine steward pranced to tableside sporting a large ornate key about his neck, which he wore as if it were the Croix de Guerre. His approval of Pine was deftly withheld pending the forthcoming order, and his manner was as impeccable as his costume.

"*Monsieur?*" he queried. Pine dipped his head in response. It seemed the only proper greeting to this formidable adversary.

"I think, with the langoustine, we shall have a Pouilly-Fumé, perhaps a '62; with the entrée, a Latour. What years do you have; the Chateau?"

"I am sorry, sir," the steward intoned, devastated by the admission. "The only year we have left is '61." He said it in a manner indicating that he did not think Pine, despite being American, should have it.

"Well then, give us something that you would recommend in a good year."

"*Oui, Monsieur,*" the steward smiled in dignified vindication. It was wise of Pine to allow the expert who knew his cellar, to make the choice.

"We will have champagne with dessert, a *Blanc de Blanc,*" Pine concluded. He would have liked to tell the steward to be sure that the Fumé was cold enough, but he did not have the nerve; the wine, he knew, would be served at precisely the correct temperature, a bit too warm for him.

Pine had not had a meal such as this in almost six years. At first he was not sure he would remember what was good, but his recollection of the excellent wines he had shared with Pam had not diminished the slightest. In fact, it was one of the things for which he was most grateful to her. She had insisted on having wine with every meal, even breakfast, although cut with water, and had trained Pine well. He had learned the Chateaux, both good and bad, for it was important to taste the bad as well, and the years that each Chateau had had its best crop. Since having left Pam, he could never afford the big wines and it was one of the few luxuries that he missed.

The steward returned with the Fumé, properly chilled. He removed the cork and laid it discreetly on the table after inconspicuously having waved it under his nose. He poured a small quantity into Pine's glass. The wine was full and clung to the glass as a film of fine transparent oil when it was tipped. Its bouquet, which was cut back by the chill, reached him as he drew in a large airy sip.

"Fine," was all he said. The wine was not known as a great one, simply a good dry white that was light enough to prepare the palate for the next, but not so light as to be tasteless.

The meal proceeded in a casual manner, each course having its own charm. The steward arrived with a '55 Chambertin, and a similar ritual was performed, but this time, Pine found the wine a bit tannic and the steward, profuse with sorow, all hands and eyebrows and shoulders despite his dignity, said he would bring another. Pine changed the order to a '59 Pommard which proved to be beautiful. It amused Pine to note that the steward had placed his first selection on the back of the bar and after sampling it, had wrinkled his nose slightly, and left the bottle standing there. The bartender, seeing the bottle rejected, poured himself a beakerful and drank it down without a change of expression, except for an unheard, but obvious burp.

For dessert they had fresh fruit in Grand Marnier with a

most excellent bottle of champagne. They decided to have coffee elsewhere, and charging the dinner on his credit card, Pine added tips for everybody, including the bartender who had pilfered the wine.

The night had become quite cold and extremely clear. Even in the city, they could see stars occasionally peeking out from behind a building. Despite the cool air, they decided to walk back to the Latin Quarter, which was no more than a mile or two from the restaurant.

The Champs-Élysées was crowded with people dressed in costume varying from formal to hippie. At ten o'clock, even on a Thursday evening in the middle of the autumn social season, Paris could be little else but busy.

Outside the exclusive and not-so-exclusive cafés, further up the Champs, they dimly heard hippie groups playing their versions of the pop music of the day on guitars and other more innovative instruments in the hope that affluent tourists would drop a franc or two in little tins wielded by long haired and sullen looking young women. An occasional gust of wind rattled remaining leaves on trees that lined this portion of the Champs, creating a much softer music. Pine felt a warm glow after the large dinner and the excellent wines. Laura snuggled deeper in the crook of his arm, hiding from the cool air and gusty breezes. They walked without speaking, each lost in his own thoughts. Their pace was rapid, but relaxed. A few dozen paces behind them, a man in a long top coat, hands stuffed in pockets, neck nestled in collar, followed discreetly. He had left a Peugeot in Avenue Marbeuf.

8

Pine and Laura stopped at a small café opposite the Theatre Odéon at the corner of Rue de Vaugirard. They had decided that hot chocolate would be more appropriate than the coffee, as the evening had turned out to be deceptively cool. Ever since Laura had checked into the Candide, something that Pine could not place had been bothering him. As they sat there, a uniformed police officer passed by and Pine realized what it was that had been troubling him.

When Laura had checked into the Candide, she had been required to fill out the police registration cards that were always filed by transients and were turned into the station house as evening came on. It struck him that she would have had to do the same at the decrepit hostel where Pine had met her. When the two dead Germans were found in the back stairwell, the police would, no doubt, question each of the residents about the incident and when they found Laura gone, they would search for her. The search would not take long, as the new card, filed by the Candide, would locate her, certainly before the next evening. The clerk at the Candide would unquestionably tie the two of them together and he would be implicated. That would mean he could not leave Paris in the morning or probably until the investigation was complete; it would also mean that in all likelihood his involvement would be discovered, since his fingerprints were spread all over the small hostel. He did not question that the Embassy, with Bigger in charge of security and obviously of some importance, would be of little service to him in the event of trouble. The complexities of the situation were increasing.

"If you looked any more contemplative," Laura began, "I'd suspect you of thinking of some other girl."

Pine explained his thoughts about the inevitable police investigation. He suggested that she might explain that they met on the plane and had made a date. When she discovered how bad the little hostel was, she decided to leave and Pine had agreed to help her find a new place. She looked a bit insulted by the suggestion.

"You really don't think that I'd squeal on you, do you?" There was something in her manner that made Pine uneasy.

"Wait a minute here." He looked carefully into her eyes. "It suddenly seems rather strange to me that you're taking this attitude. Naturally, I don't expect you to squeal, as you put it, but after all, how often do your gentlemen friends go around killing muggers, and you in the backseat? It just seems to me that you're taking this all a little *too* well."

Laura gazed at him with half a smile on her lips.

"I mean, after all, if I saw a guy kill two people in front of my eyes that very afternoon, I wouldn't be sitting so calmly discussing the question of squealing with him as you are. What is it that makes you think that the story I told you was true? What kind of girl are you anyway? Even murder in self-defense is a homicide and though there may be a claim of justification, there would have to be a hearing to determine that."

"Okay, then," she replied, with a broader smirk. "I'll squeal, if that's what you want."

"That's not at all what I want, and you know it. Tell me what's going on in that circuitous little head of yours?"

"Well, *you* asked me, don't forget. First of all, I don't believe that little fairy tale you told me this evening before dinner, at least not all of it. Secondly, your behavior has been rather strange regarding all this secrecy, and personally, I think that you *are* a spy."

Pine cringed and looked around as she said the last. A man in a long top coat, sitting a few tables away also looked up

"Now you know that's ridiculous. A spy! My God—and you talk about fairy tales."

"Well, that's what I think. You asked me, remember?" Laura picked up her cup and finished the dregs of dark chocolate that lined the bottom.

Pine left money on the table and escorted her out to the street again. As they left, the man in the top coat called for his check.

It was just past twelve-thirty when Pine got back to his room with Laura. Putting the oversized door key into the gross lock, he turned to catch her staring at him with obvious desire. The door opened and the light from the hallway fell slantwise into the room. There appeared to be some clutter on the floor near the door and Pine, pushing the door hard against it to enter, stepped in, switching on the noisy knob that controlled the overhead lights.

The room looked as if it had been attacked by vandals. The drawers were all open with clothing hanging over edges and scattered about the floor. The bed had been turned over, the mattress slit, the stuffing oozing from the slashes like pus. Pillows had been fully deflated, feathers strewn everywhere, and the closet and cupboards had been swept bare; Pine's suitcase had been dumped and the lining cut out. In addition, the window was agape, and the room was cold. In the bathroom, Pine's shaving equipment had been messed up and the little transistor radio he had left by the tub had had its back removed.

Laura stood there wide-eyed and surveyed the mess. Pine walked over to her and put his arm around her shoulders.

"I'll just collect my clothes and have the clerk give me another room for the night." Picking up the house phone, Pine called the clerk and asked him to come up to the room.

He arrived after perhaps ten minutes, and Pine had already got most of his clothing stuffed into the ruptured suitcase. The clerk looked briefly at the condition of the room, and after an accusing glare at Pine, began to complain vociferously in extremely rapid French. Pine guessed that Laura understood; he did not. Finally cooling down a bit, the clerk asked what had happened.

"Well, if I knew that, I wouldn't have asked you up here," Pine replied sharply. Actually, he had a good idea what had happened and although it scared him badly, he was glad that he had taken the list with him to dinner. "I don't think anything was stolen, so I won't file a complaint, but I do expect the hotel to replace my luggage and I certainly can't sleep here tonight."

The clerk looked carefully at Pine from under dark thick brows. Glancing first at the bed and then at Laura, he said:

"We have no vacancy. Perhaps . . ." His unfinished sentence was punctuated by a shrug towards Laura. She restrained a grin and turned away from the men.

"See here," he continued. "I can do nothing tonight, *Monsieur.*" He was definitive. "Tomorrow I will have a new mattress and pillow brought up, and we will clean the room for you. Until then there is no one to do the work." His contrition was professional and it was obvious that he could not have cared less. Pine had an almost uncontrollable urge to shove the desk clerk into the night-table drawer.

"Why don't you come up to my room for now?" Laura said after the clerk had left. "We really can't talk here." She repressed another grin.

Pine strode to the window and slammed the two swinging sections together; the catch was not working properly and the window remained slightly ajar. As he returned to Laura, he took a swipe with his foot at a pile of stuffing that protruded from the mattress. The force of his kick tumbled the ruined pad more fully upon the floor so that only a portion of it remained on the bed frame; white, fluffy filling shot into the air, and a small ball of stuffing landed on Laura's nose.

Grabbing a handful of down from one of the pillows, Laura flung it at Pine, succeeding only in scattering a flurry of softness into the air as though snow had started to fall in the small room. With a wide grin, she reached for another handful of feathers, but Pine, who was now beginning to laugh, leaped over the clutter on the floor between them and grasped her arm before she could toss them. The force of his motion knocked Laura to her knees and Pine, unable to stop himself, fell over her, landing on his back with his feet against the wall.

In the moment it took for them to squirm after each other to prevent another onslaught of feathers, the humor of the situation dispersed. Pine found himself lying on a pile of scattered rags, ruined bedding and rumpled clothing with Laura stretched across his body, her right arm held high in his left hand, her hand slowly releasing its load of feathers and mattress filling.

"I think we'd better get out of here, Mark," she said, trying not to look too intently into his eyes.

Pine resisted her first attempt to rise, and pulled her more fully on top of him. Slipping his arm behind her back, he pulled her toward his lips and kissed her gently on the side of her mouth. Laura tried to turn her head away from him, but Pine fought her efforts and kissed her again, more strongly, this time on the lips. At first she resisted, and after a few moments relaxed slightly as the emotion began to encompass her.

Without quite realizing how they had moved, Pine found himself over her body, his elbows supporting his weight, her arms loosely about his neck as she lay on her back. The bare floor was cold and hard, and feathers and particles of fluff were still drifting lazily in the air, floating down to coat them. Pine brushed a feather away from Laura's cheek and kissed her where the feather had rested. He then kissed her other cheek, her chin, her lips.

"I don't think we should be doing this," Laura said with a distracted look. She was beginning to lose her resolve and knew that if she did not stop him at this point, it would be impossible to do so later. "Mark," she said. "Please let me up." Her voice did not carry conviction.

Pine did nothing. He lay there looking at her and did not move. In a sudden movement, he pulled her against him roughly and pressed her lips tightly to his in a long, passionate kiss; her response was almost immediate and equally forceful. Reaching down to her shoulder, Pine slid the black dress over and kissed her shoulder where it joined her neck. Laura lifted her chin and closed her eyes as he worked his lips lower. As she shifted her position, her hair became undone and cascaded about his neck; he could smell her perfume.

Raising her body, Pine undid the zipper at the back of the dress. It fell gently forward, revealing a tiny, fragile black bra. Pine slipped his thumb under the clasp at the back and almost as if by his touch, the garment snapped open and dropped to her lap. Pine felt self-conscious, but he could not stop staring at her breasts. They were small, but full and firm, and they were moving softly with each short breath that she took.

Laura rose suddenly and slipped the dress down over her hips. She stood there for a moment, wearing nothing but black bikini panties and a garter belt that held her stockings. Pine leaned over and kissed the bare skin above the stocking tops. Laura pulled him to his feet and placed both arms about his neck, and with her body pressed tightly against his she kissed him with an ardor that belied her former coyness.

By the time Pine had shed his clothing, Laura was lying naked on the shredded mattress which she had pulled onto the floor. Standing over her as she lay in the dim light, Pine could see the goose bumps that covered her arms in the cold room. Her body was narrow and the softness of her skin was emphasized by the firmness beneath it. As he bent to her, she reached out to him and smiled.

After about an hour, Pine lifted himself to his feet and readjusted his bandage.

"Mr. Pine has certainly had an hectic day," he said, looking about the ravaged chamber, letting his eyes once more fall upon the woman who lay at his feet grinning.

The two dressed hurriedly in the cold.

"I'll take you up on the offer of your room," he said. Laura laughed and headed towards the door.

She preceded him up the one flight, forsaking the anti-quated elevator. But as Pine entered her room, he began to feel a detachment and an unreasonable irritability growing within him. Perhaps it was the accumulated tension of the day, or the uncertainty of events, but when Laura said,

"Why don't you tell me what's going on here?" he said,

"Look, why don't you mind your own business!" He was sorry before he had finished the sentence, but the damage had been done, the mood of the evening broken.

Laura huffed to the other end of the room and spun around, her lower lip tightly clasped between her teeth.

"Okay Mister," she snapped. "If you don't want my help, you can go to hell! I didn't ask to be pulled into your mess; it was your idea. Why don't you leave *me* alone." With which she slammed herself into the bathroom, shutting Pine out.

Wanting to say something, but not being able to think of what, Pine walked back down to his room and attempted to rearrange the bed so that it would be usable. Finally getting it into a reasonable shape, he again stripped down to his underwear and flopped upon the sagging pallet. He was asleep almost before his body had sunk fully into the ruined padding.

Pine dreamt that his mouth was stuffed up; he awoke with his mouth stuffed up. In addition, his hands were tied behind his back and his feet were trussed up behind him. All in all, it was a very undignified position. The odor of chloroform still lingered and Pine's head felt as if someone had scraped out his brains with a garden trowel. Every time he tried to move, his sore shoulder throbbed incessantly and the cut on his arm had reopened and was bleeding. The rest of him did not feel too much better.

Looking around the room, he saw that it had been ransacked again, and then, looking towards the bathroom, from which sounds were emerging, he saw that it was still being ransacked. Two men were working feverishly, tearing up the little room, obviously in search of something; Pine well knew what they were searching for. The men were speaking to each other in what sounded to Pine like Russian. He wished his mouth were free so that he could ask permission to use the toilet.

One of the men came out and saw that his eyes were open, and walking over to him, smiled. The Russian ripped off the tape covering his mouth and pulled out the cloth gag. Instead of being polite and introducing himself, the Russian hit Pine sharply across the face with an open hand. It hurt a lot; almost as much as the tape that had been ripped off.

"Where is the list?" He hit Pine three more times to make sure he got the point. Pine got the point.

"I don't know what you're talking about." He could be stubborn too, he hoped.

"Mister Pine. We can't play games with you." The accent was sinister. Pine wondered if that was because all the spy movies he had seen had had sinister Russian inquisitors. "If you do not tell us, we will cause you a great deal of pain."

"Listen, fella." Pine's courage had begun to flag, but he figured that he would try a little longer. "If I had anything that you wanted you can be sure I'd give it to you." The Russian gave it to Pine.

He pulled him upright and ripped off his few remaining garments. Then the Russian threw Pine's nude body on the floor and started to kick him with his heavy boots. After about five kicks, it stopped hurting, and Pine felt himself drift as though he were drugged. He came back to awareness when he was pulled back to his knees, and slapped a few more times. That was when the stomping began to hurt.

The Russian brought his foot squarely into Pine's groin and Pine, his breath driven sharply out, tears smarting in his eyes, fell over seeing nothing but red and black flashes. He never in his life felt such searing, shocking pain and could not understand why he did not faint. He tried to talk. He tried to say that he would talk. But nothing came out. A guy could get killed this way, he thought over the pain; worse, maybe he would not die. Then he vomited and thought that he would drown in the vomit as he tried to catch his breath that was still fighting the contracted stomach muscles. The kick in the groin scared him badly. He tried to get a word out, to give

73

in, to speak, but his tongue would not respond to the command.

The two Russians manhandled him into a chair and cut the ropes that bound him. Knocking him back with a chop to his cheek, one of the men said something to the other in their language.

"Do you want more of this, Pine?" Pine did not want any of it. But he still could not catch his breath or speak. Shaking his head emphatically, he gasped large gulps of air that refused to enter his lungs. One of the Russians got some water and splashed it in Pine's face. Then they sat down on the bed to wait until Pine could speak again.

It took about ten pain-racked minutes for the agony to subside sufficiently to make it possible to utter even a grunt. He made them to understand that the paper they wanted was in his inside jacket pocket. One of the men grabbed the jacket and looked; it was not there. Moving back threateningly toward Pine, he saw the genuine shock in Pine's face at the missing document and returned to the closet where the jacket had been hung. The envelope had been wedged between the door and the jamb near the hinge and must have fallen out of the pocket when the jacket was so rudely pulled from the hanger. A quick examination proved it to be what they sought.

By now, Pine had got some breath back, although he was still a complete package of pain; he was surprised to recognize that the mewling that he had been hearing had been coming from him and he made an effort to be quiet. His groin, he was sure, would be a mass of jelly when he got the nerve to look down there. At any rate, he was sure that his usefulness to the female of the species was permanently terminated. He wanted to die. The second Russian pulled a large curved knife from his jacket. Walking over to Pine, he pulled his head back by his hair, making his intent rather clear. Pine let out a scream that literally rocked the window glass in the room, finding the air to generate the noise from somewhere deep in his gut; apparently he did not want to die. The two men hesitated a moment and then took immediate flight. Pine's last thoughts before he passed out were: one, that's all for fairy book ideas of subtle torture; and two, very unprofessional; they should have killed him.

9

Pine woke up in bed, covered with a blanket. He did not remember getting into bed, but remembered rather well the cruel beating he had sustained. The water was rushing in the sink and after a moment, Laura came over to him with a glass in one hand and a wet towel in the other. Looking past her towards his watch on the bed table, he saw that it was three-thirty.

"I heard you scream. What happened here; who were those men?" She was extremely upset.

Pine diverted his eyes from the small ominous puddle on the floor near the chair; he still felt an excrutiating pain in his groin.

"Two men," he managed inanely. "They must have chloroformed me while I was asleep." There was a small pad of gauze on the floor near the bed, but all odor had dissipated. "How did I get back into the bed?" he asked as he took a drink of the water.

Laura gently wiped his face with the damp towel, attempting to stop the flow of blood that ran freely from his injuries. She explained that she had been unable to sleep after their argument and had come down to speak with him. As she approached his door, she had heard his scream. She entered the room as quickly as possible and saw two men leaving through the window, one of whom had been standing over Pine with a knife in his hand. Pine had fallen from the chair and was lying naked on the floor, covered with blood. She thought he was dead until he stirred and was sick on the floor at the foot of the chair. Pine stopped casting sidewise glances towards the small puddle near the chair; he felt considerably more hopeful now respecting the condition of his groin.

Helping him onto the bed, she continued, she had covered him and gone to the sink for water and something to clean him up with.

"Look Mark," she stated simply, after finishing her explanation. "I know that this may be none of my business, but you seem to be getting into more trouble every minute. Can't I help you in any way? Can't you tell me what it's all about?"

Pine then remembered that the list had been taken from him. Who would believe his story about Bigger now that he had no proof to display? He also felt that Laura, after all she had been through with him, was entitled to know a bit more than he had already told her.

"Let me think for a moment, Laura," he said. "I have to get this new developement clear in my mind first."

Deplint's sister had been the only person who knew that he had had the list and she was dead. She had obviously not told Bigger and his Germans anything that afternoon before they had killed her or Pine would not have got away so easily, as they would have continued the search for him until they had found him.

Bigger and the two Germans had attempted to obtain the list for whatever reasons they had. Now two Russians had assaulted him and got the list. In addition, earlier that evening, the room had been searched by other parties unknown. It all meant that there were at least two groups seeking the intelligence and one of them did not know that the other had succeeded. He assumed that there had been two groups because the first group had already searched in places that the Russians had spent considerable time and effort on, and had they been there before, the Russians would not have bothered to check those places again, at least to the extent that they did. Pine wondered how so many different people had known that he was involved in this pick-up. If Bigger were in business for himself, then additional leaks in security were not beyond possibility. The one thing he could not surmise was which of the two groups Bigger belonged to; and was it Bigger's group that had got the list from him in the end?

The Russians now had got what they wanted. But the other group had not, and unfortunately, they did not know that the Russians had been successful. Pine was, therefore, sure that the first group would be back for another attempt. He was also bothered that the Russians had wanted to kill him, for which there could be no reason, unless he knew something that had to be quieted. Also, Laura's entrance into the room had interrupted them, or Pine would have been dead. Obviously, their primary job was to get the list to whomever they worked for. They could always return to finish Pine later if they so intended.

The more Pine thought about it the worse his head felt. Looking at Laura, Pine made his decision. He told her everything that had happened from his meeting in New York with Bigger and related his conclusions as he conceived them.

Laura sat quietly throughout the story and when Pine had finished, she was looking deeply into his eyes.

"Is that the complete truth?"

"Yes," Pine answered simply. "Everything,"

"I believe you." She was very quiet now. "It's almost incredible. You couldn't have made that one up. My God!" she suddenly exploded. "You *are* a spy after all!"

"Yes, I guess I am, of sorts." He grinned sheepishly, painfully conscious that his face was stiffening.

"How much more spyish can you *get?*" She walked over and sat by him on the damaged bed where he had now propped himself into a sitting position. He felt that she was more taken with the romance of the situation than with his seriousness.

The blanket had fallen off his shoulders and lay about his waist. His entire left side was raw and bruised from the stomping, but when he breathed deeply, he did not get that sharp feeling that usually presages a broken rib. His body was covered with drying blood, and his arm, although clotting again, was red and angry. Laura continued working on Pine's body, never once looking at his face for fear that she would see his grimaces of pain. When she had cleaned him from head to waist, she suggested that he retire to the bathroom to finish the job himself on his lower body. She helped him rise and led him to the sink; the pain in his groin was so intense that it was almost all she could do to guide his naked quivering body in the right direction. After washing, he got back to the bed by himself, a major feat, and she covered him with a blanket. Despite the pain, he fell immediately into a fitful sleep.

The sun was streaming into the room through a slit in the thin drapes that hung by the partly open window. Pine awakened in pain, recalling the past night's events. Laura was sleeping in one of the chairs, and her bathrobe had fallen open during the night. Seeing her in nothing but a flimsy pair of black bikini panties, Pine was relieved to discover his fears of emasculation the night before had been unfounded.

He groaned himself off the bed and onto his feet. Actually, he did not feel much worse than he had felt after the first day of football practice back in his high school days, except for the shooting pains in his groin and stomach. But he knew that as they healed, the pains would get worse.

Limping to Laura's side as quietly as his aching bones and muscles would let him, he reached down to pull the end of the bathrobe over her body. But as he did so, his foot found the little pool of sickness on the floor and out it slid. Thrown off balance, and not exactly feeling athletic, he toppled over onto Laura, slamming his jaw bone deeply into her abdomen. Laura leaped into the air emitting a sharp gasp, and it was all over in a second with Pine slithering down onto the floor at her feet. Laura wrapped the bathrobe tightly around her body and looked down at Pine's naked body.

"Well, I guess that that little escapade last night did nothing to inhibit your libido, did it?"

"I thought I'd have got back into bed before you awakened. I mean . . . look," he stammered. "All I was trying to do was cover you up. You see . . ."

Her laughter interrupted his sentence.

"Don't bother to explain," she declared with a broad grin. "Let me imagine the worst about you. It's more interesting."

Suddenly conscious of his own nakedness, Pine wrapped himself in the damp towel that lay by the chair. Walking to the pile of clothes on the floor near the closet, he stooped down, uttering a groan, and quietly slipped into a pair of pants. Laura had meanwhile started to pick up some of the litter on the floor. Crossing to the puddle near the chair, Pine dropped the towel over it and went on to open the window wider. Then he sat down on the edge of the bed with a sigh and looked at Laura.

"I guess the best thing now is to act innocent and call Bigger. It will be interesting to note his reaction to my call. What time do you make it?"

"It's about nine-thirty." She picked up his watch from the other side of the bed and walked it over to him.

Picking up the phone near the bed, Pine dialed the Embassy. While he was waiting, it occurred to him that Bigger might not be in yet and if he left a name, it would destroy any attempt to get some reaction out of him. Before he could decide to hang up and try again later, Bigger's secretary answered the call. Trying to disguise his voice so that if Bigger were out, he could leave a false name, he asked to speak with Mr. Bigger.

"I'm sorry, Mr. Pine. It is Mr. Pine, isn't it? What's the matter with your voice this morning? Mr. Bigger is not in right now. Do you want to leave . . . Oh, wait a moment, he just arrived."

Pine figured that Bigger might not know about the successful attack last night if he were working with the first team of searchers, in which case it might be wise to tell him, to prevent another assault from him. But then he realized that if Bigger had engineered the successful raid, he would know that Pine had lied to him about getting the list in the first place which would make it obvious to Bigger that his cover was blown. In the same respect, if he admitted that he had had the list that was stolen, it would have the same effect, since Bigger would again know that Pine had withheld the information from him. In either case, Bigger would be on to Pine, and that would be extremely dangerous. Pine was sorry he had called so precipitously before he had made his plans and considered the consequences. But now it was too late.

"How are you this morning, Pine?" Bigger seemed quite cheerful. "Listen, I don't see any reason why you can't return to New York today if you wish." Bigger had his own plans for

Pine and it made little difference to him what Pine did. Sending him home would make it easy to find him, as he would be either at the airport later that day, or at least in predictable places. It was better than roaming about Paris.

"Mr. Bigger," Pine interjected on impulse. "I've got something to tell you. I was assaulted last night by two men who sounded like Russians. They beat me up badly and ransacked my place here." Pine listened carefully to the reply.

"Why that's terrible, Mr. Pine. I'm awfully sorry about that." Bigger sounded most sincere. "I hope nothing got broken, on you, I mean. We really blew this deal and I'm sorry that you had to suffer for it."

Pine was astounded that Bigger had not remonstrated on how Russians or any other persons had got wind of Pine's role in the delivery of the intelligence.

"You were lucky that Miss Kennedy came into the room when she did . . ." Bigger caught himself too late. There was only one way that he could have known about Laura's intervention, or for that matter, about Laura at all.

Nine o'clock in the morning is not the best time for many people to have to think quickly. There were a few moments of silence at both ends of the line. Bigger recovered first; he hung up. That was his second mistake, because now Pine knew.

Bigger had been terribly upset when he had heard from his team that Pine had had the message, and had not been killed. That Pine had refused to turn the intelligence over to him earlier indicated that he knew something about Bigger, but he still did not know how much Pine knew. The possibility that Pine had killed both Otto and Hans had occurred to him, but he had dismissed that thought as improbable; they were professionals and Pine was not. He knew that other agents were looking for the list and had assumed that another street

82

man had found the Germans and taken them out while they were awaiting Pine.

Bigger cursed the agents who had retrieved the list, but had left Pine alive. Their instructions were to kill him if the list was there because then, Bigger knew, Pine had to be on to him. And then on the phone, Bigger had to make that stupid slip. And then to make matters worse, he had cut the connection on the phone. Actually, it made little difference. Pine knew, and that was that. Pine had to be killed, and quickly. His people would have to be told that Pine was on alert and not simply headed for the airport. Bigger picked up the phone.

Rising from the bed with more vigor than he thought he could muster, Pine grabbed Laura by the shoulder.

"We've got to get out of here fast."

"What happened?" she asked as Pine was dragging out his bag so that he could pack. He tossed his clothes into the suitcase, ripping off pieces of lining that hung from the sides, and indiscriminately kept out enough to serve him for the day. Pulling Laura after him to the door, a shirt and a suit draped over his arm, he pushed her into the hall and up the stairs to her room.

Once there, he explained what had happened and that they had to get out of the area as soon as possible. He knew it would not be long before Bigger's goons came back for him and for her, as they now suspected her involvement. Pine wanted to dress quickly and get out, but Laura pointed out that he had a great deal of dried blood on him and anyone who saw him would not easily forget the disheveled and bloody American in unmatching clothes. Americans just did not travel that way.

With misgivings, Pine jumped into a quick hot bath to rid himself of the blood and grime. The hot water soothed his pains somewhat and he felt much better thereafter. Laura had repacked his bag and got herself ready to leave. She had also selected an outfit for him that matched, so that he would not be too conspicuous. As Pine dressed, she put the last touches on herself. Incredibly, within fifteen minutes, they were ready to leave the hotel.

Taking the stairs so not to be observed, they emerged at the end of the lobby, bags in hand. Hoping not to be seen, they slunk towards the front door keeping as many people between them and the desk clerk as they could. Didn't that guy ever sleep, thought Pine, as a sullen French voice called out to him,

"*Monsieur* Pine, *Monsieur* Pine. You are not leaving? You do not let a little inconvenience like last night bother you?"

Pine did not bother to answer. Grabbing Laura, he lit out like the proverbial fox at a hunt, and continued on until they hit the Boul' Mich' at the corner of Rue de Vaugirard. Hailing a cab, Pine shoved the girl and the bags in and climbed stiffly over the clutter to sit at Laura's right. In English, slowly and distinctly, he instructed the cabbie to drive them around Paris until otherwise directed. As Pine had hoped, the driver did not understand what he said. Further proof was secured when no response was received from the driver after a few well chosen insults related to him and his mother. Repeating the request politely in French, Pine sat back to discuss the problem with Laura as the cab pulled out. He had plans to make and he knew not where to begin.

10

Bigger's men reported later that morning that Pine had left the hotel before they could get to him and that the American girl had gone with him. Bigger's panic was growing. He knew that Pine would not, could not, come to the Embassy in Paris, but that would not stop him from going to another country. Bigger's entire career lay in the balance, and if Pine had read and could recall any of the data on the list, more than Bigger's career would suffer. Indeed, the Russians were less gentle with failure than the Americans.

Bigger had to get Pine. But how? The solution was so simple that when he thought of it, Bigger began to shake with amusement. The French police were, no doubt, investigating the death of the two Germans who had been left at the drop in Rue de Vaugirard. It would be easy to have an anonymous caller advise the Prefecture of Police of Pine's and the girl's complicity. Since Pine had had the list, he must have got it from the Deplint woman; that meant that he had been in the building at nine Rue de Vaugirard and had probably left fingerprints on the railings and God knew where else. With the tip that Pine was involved at that building and the present flight without explanation from his hotel, the police would have to check it out; they surely had few leads, as it was. Fingerprints would seal his fate. After he had been arrested, it would be easy for Bigger to reach and silence him, since, as an Embassy official, he would have easy access to Pine. How he would arrange Pine's death was something he would work out later. The Prefecture would establish a net and perhaps that would prevent Pine from leaving the city; if not, certainly, the country. Pine's ravings about Bigger, if any, would be certainly discounted.

Bigger called the central office of the Prefecture and the duty sergeant switched him to a detective who was assigned to the case.

"Ah Monsieur, you have no idea how helpful you are to us," the policeman remarked after Bigger, speaking through his handkerchief, dropped his information. "We know that Ma'amselle Kennedy, she is missing from *numero neuf* Rue de Vaugirard, but now you tell us about Monsieur Pine who brings her to the Hotel Candide. Ah, it begins all to fit, how you say, like the glove in the hand." The detective sounded exactly like Charles Boyer. "Could you give us your name, please?" he continued.

Bigger rang off without answering. He had not realized how deeply Pine had implicated himself; he was pleased. The police would contact the Embassy as a matter of course, when Pine was captured, and Bigger left word that he was to be notified immediately when this occurred. He hoped that his contact Boris would be similarly pleased, although he doubted it. Boris was never pleased.

After having searched Pine's room earlier in the evening and found nothing, Packer telephoned the Bureau to report. He was told to keep a tail on Pine. Packer reflected that the trouble with working for the Intelligence Service in France was that it paid less than the regular police, but required longer hours; and if one succeeded in accomplishing something of note, he got no recognition, which of course meant no raise. Packer sent a man to get some cheese and a loaf of bread that had become stale in the few hours since it had been baked, and sipped away at a paper cup of wine from a bottle of inexpensive *onze degree* that he purchased in the grocery across from the hotel where he waited.

In the morning, when Pine and the girl left the hotel with their baggage, Packer, who was about to go off duty, noted the cab's number and phoned in to have the vehicle followed. He was informed that they had identified the two dead men in Rue de Vaugirard, who turned out to be Soviet agents of East German nationality, and that the girl who had been missing from that building had moved to the Candide and was apparently the woman with whom Pine had spent the evening and with whom he had left that morning. Packer went home to get some sleep.

The Chief called the central offices of the Prefecture in Paris and was rather surprised to learn that they already knew of Pine's escape and of his complicity in the apparent homicides. They agreed grudgingly to keep Intelligence informed of their progress in the case and of Pine's location. It was a sorry state of affairs, he reflected, when Intelligence learned things after the local police. The Chief's mood was considerably blacker for the rest of the day.

As the cab cruised towards the Bois de Bologne, Pine decided on a course of action. Opening Laura's smaller overnight bag, he removed its contents and put in a few changes of clothes from both his luggage and from Laura's other bag. Then, stuffing the discarded clothing into his almost empty case, he instructed the driver to take them to a Turkish bath that he knew in one of the better districts of Paris. When they arrived, Pine gave Laura the overnight bag and disappeared into the building with the two larger cases. He stepped out shortly thereafter, empty handed.

"What's up now?" Laura asked. She had paid the cabbie and sent it away.

"We had to get rid of all that luggage. It was too cumbersome. We have enough stuff in this small bag of yours to keep us going for a while." Laura seemed dubious.

"How much money do you have on you, Laura?" Pine was digging into his practically empty pockets.

"Let's see. About two hundred fifty francs and three hundred dollars in traveller's cheques."

"That's good. I have only twenty five francs, about five dollars. I don't think I can cash a check here in Paris even at American Express. Say! What about American Express? Let's get over there now. I can get three hundred dollars from them on my credit card. Between us we'll have enough to get along on until we can figure out our next step."

They caught the Metro at Trocadero towards Marie de Montreuil and changed at Franklin D. Roosevelt and again at Concorde. It was only one more stop on the line towards Charenton-Ecoles. Getting out at Opera they walked across the street to the large building that housed the offices of American Express. Fighting their way through the thick crowd of tourists, students, and business people, they made their way over to the cashier's desks.

Pine took his three hundred dollars in francs, and Laura exchanged her traveller's cheques for cash. They took the money, half in francs, half in American dollars; traveller's cheques were fine, but they left a trail that Bigger might have been able to follow; Pine was trying to be as careful as he could. It was now ten-thirty. Since neither had eaten and since they had no other place to go, they checked the single valise at the luggage counter and crossed over past the Opera building, to a small restaurant where "American hamburgers" were supposedly served.

Pine did not know what to do next. He knew that they would have to find a place to hole-up, but he realized that any hotel would require police registration through which Bigger, with his Embassy authority, could probably trace them. The solution was to get a car, drive out of the city, and find a small country farm house where the owner, with proper financial encouragement, would let a "honeymooning couple" spend a few nights. Then after a few days, when their trail had cooled a bit, they could get a train to, say, Amsterdam, or some other location where the American Embassy would be friendlier. He told Laura his idea and she agreed that it seemed the best procedure to follow.

"Why Mark Pine," a familiar voice greeted. "How the fuck are ya? What are you doing here in Paris?" Even though Pine recognized the voice, or rather the mode of address, there was a brief moment during which he felt his heart stop; in his present circumstances, he did not expect to hear his name called so loudly.

Looking up at a man about his own age, shorter, slightly balding, spreading at the waist and grinning at Pine broadly, he recognized a former classmate of his from M.I.T. He had not been close friends with him, but he had often heard his characteristic greeting, one for which he had been famous when Pine knew him: how-the-fuck-are-ya?

"Charlie Blegg?" Pine really did not want to see anyone now, but he would be polite and not cause a scene. "Why sure. How have you been?"

"Not bad, not bad, old man." Pine did not know whether

Blegg was referring to him or to Laura, whom he was measuring with a leer that proclaimed him married too long.

"I'm living here in Paris now, you know. Got a position with a very good electronics firm, in fact. Say! I heard that you went into law? Couldn't take the rough stuff, huh?" The last was said with a kidding-around-but-I-really-mean-it grin. Old "Blech" hadn't changed much, except in appearance.

"Can't stay long and talk," he said. "Wife and me, we're going to Rome this afternoon for a three week business trip. Not bad, eh old man?" Pine's mind began to work fast.

"Why good ol' Charlie Blegg appearing out of nowhere after ten years and he thinks that I'm going to let him get away from me without a drink or something? Not on your life. After all, Charlie, weren't we almost best friends at Tech back in the good ol' days, old boy?" Laura looked at Pine as if he had suddenly contracted leprosy and his nose had fallen into her soup. Blegg grinned even more widely. "Come on, sit down. Have one drink with my wife and me." This time Laura really looked at Pine.

"So you got hooked, too, ha, ha? No offense meant, Mrs. Pine. Well, it looks like you did pretty well for yourself, old man."

"Where do you live in Paris, Charlie?"

"Oh, we live over in the Sixteenth. Corner of Avenue Mozart near Jasmine. Pretty soft, eh old man?" It *was* a prime area, in fact, one of the best.

"You know, Charlie, old man, Laura and I have a problem. We just got married a few days ago, and this is our honeymoon." Charlie began to glow.

"We've got a friend at the Embassy here, small job, nothing important, and all he wants to do is throw parties for us. I guess it makes him feel important. Well, you know, we'd like to get away by ourselves for a while, but every time we check into a new hotel, he finds us through the Embassy. He thinks we're playing games with him. Knowing Paris as you probably do, you'd be in a good position to advise us where to go where we didn't have to register with the police, or something."

"Is that so? Say! I've got an idea!" Pine looked at him with the innocence of a babe. Charlie looked as if he had just invented the safety pin.

"Listen to Charlie, dear," Pine said, turning to Laura with a wink. "He's got an idea."

"Why don't you stay at my place for a few days?" His hand was already in his pocket for the keys. Pine felt a stab of guilt; Charlie may have had a few bad habits, but he was always a generous and kindly chap.

"Oh no, Charlie, I couldn't do that." Laura kicked him under the table. "It would be too much trouble for you. Besides your wife wouldn't like it."

"The hell. What are old classmates for anyway, Mark, old man?" You say black, Charlie says white, every time. "No, I really couldn't, Charlie."

"If you don't I'll really be insulted. Here's the key. When you're through, leave it with the super." Taking out a piece of paper, he scribbled down the address and apartment number. "My wife and I are leaving in about an hour, but our bags are already out at the airport. You can move in whenever you want."

Just then, a bitchy-looking, fattish woman came up to the table and grabbed Charlie's shoulder.

"C'mon, will ya? We'll be late for the plane." She did not even see the other two.

"Sweety, let me introduce you to my best college chum, Mark Pine, and his bride Laura. This is Constance. I've given them the keys to the apartment, dear. They're on a honeymoon and don't have a place to stay."

"You what!! Well, I don't know about *that!*" She looked at Pine and Laura as if she had suddenly recalled that she had not paid the insurance premium on her silver.

Before she could fully express her objections, Charlie

pulled her away from the table, after wishing Pine the best, and headed over towards the Opera to get a cab from the line at the stand. It looked as if the Riot Act was being read to him in no uncertain terms. Pine felt like a bastard. Charlie was okay, even if he was a little pushy.

They retrieved their bags from the American Express office and then from the Turkish bath, and cabbed over to Charlie's apartment. The building was one of those solid conservative structures with two apartments on each floor to either side of the open-caged elevator. Entering, they found themselves in a large foyer in which a long mirror-topped table stood against the wall. Ahead was a long hall that shot rooms off to the right. Pine had to admit that Charlie's wife had pretty good taste: the large living room was done less formally than the hallway and foyer, and the couchs and chairs were beautifully uphol-stered. The carpeting alone must have cost more than Pine had earned in his entire working life. There was a dining room, three bedrooms, two baths and a single toilet annexed to one of the bathrooms, but separate in its own little closet. The kitchen was behind the foyer and was filled with modern American equipment. There was also a little breakfast room next to the kitchen and a balcony that overlooked Avenue Mozart. All in all, it was the last word in Parisian luxury.

Laura made herself right at home; Pine turned on an expen-sive hi-fi unit and dropped into a deep chair. It was almost two o'clock in the afternoon and the last chords of a Rachmaninoff piano concerto was still ringing in his ears when the news came on. Because he was only half listening, he did not become fully aware of anything special until he heard his own name and Laura's mentioned on the broadcast. Laura, how-ever, had been listening from inside, and came dashing into the room in a state of agitation. She explained to Pine, who was not fluent enough to pick up the broadcast in midstream, that they were both being sought by the police for questioning respecting two men who were found dead at nine Rue de Vaugirard the previous day. Checking his watch, Pine was relieved to see that Charlie would have already left Paris and would probably not hear of this for a while.

This last development was almost too much for Pine to take. Not only were the Russians looking to kill him for Bigger, but now the French police were after him for murder. And he had involved Laura. In fact, the American authorities would also be out to help the French police and avoid a nasty international scene. With every moment, Pine's spirits sank lower.

In addition, his body was beginning to stiffen up again and his ribs and shoulder ached. The cut on his arm was red and irritated, but he did not think it was infected. Laura was the only saving grace. She put aside all matters of state and ran a hot bath for him. As he lowered himself into the tub, the hot water smarting as it ran into open cuts and bruises, he heard Laura clattering around in the kitchen.

"Would you rather have steak or chicken for dinner tonight?" she called.

Pine smiled as he lay in the water. Women were wonderful; French beef was not.

"Chicken!" he called back.

11

Charles Blegg was the kind of man who would do anything for a friend. However, the motives for his generosity were not as high minded as Charlie had convinced himself they were. Throughout his life, he had done all he could for others, giving of himself in the true Christian spirit, never looking for return in this life, certainly never looking for return in any other. But if Charlie had thought about it for a moment with the concentration he devoted to tensor analysis and relativistic radiation theory, he would have seen that all his charitability was directed to acquiring praise and a recognition of his good nature. Charlie was a very good engineer; Charlie was also a very insecure person.

When Charlie's flight was delayed for technical reasons, he took the inconvenience with his usual evenness of temper despite his wife's mumblings about inefficient French industries. Charlie's wife had never developed the tolerance that Charlie had affected. Retiring to the small airport cocktail lounge, the couple took a table next to a well-dressed germanic type who wore on his shoulder a complex German camera, and in his pocket, a small transistor radio. At the moment, he was playing with the camera and listening to the radio that was tuned to the local news. Much to Charlie's horror, he heard the name of his friend Mark Pine most unflatteringly mentioned on the broadcast, together with the name of a lady who was accompanying him, whose last name was definitely not Pine.

Charlie's first reaction was envy that Pine was shacked-up with such a hot number; second, that good ol' Mark had thought to deceive by introducing her as his wife; third, and most noted, that he might be harboring a murderer in his apartment, which fact did not overly impress Charlie, since as a scientist, he considered himself above such mundane matters as civil obedience and legalistic ethics. But his most emphatic reaction was generated by the harping of his wife, who had also heard the broadcast, and was now demanding that they go to the authorities. She also reminded Charlie, and he was sure that she would be reminding him for many weeks to come, that she had suspected Pine of being up to no good when first they had met.

Charlie was torn between his wife's insistence and the potential embarassment if Pine were to be arrested upon his information. Considering the inconvenience that a postponement of his trip would entail, he was convinced by the announcement that his flight was ready to depart. Assuring his wife that he would contact the authorities as soon as they reached Rome, the Bleggs proceeded towards Gate Four as directed.

It was gray and dreary in Washington, where three men

were sitting around a rectangular table which had deteriorated into a cigarette-scarred and briefcase-scuffed battlefield. At the head of the table sat Percival Diver; to his right was Rudolph King, and opposite King was a tall man who had the enviable appearance of uncommon good looks and intelligence. He was the Chief of Security attached to the American Embassy in Paris; his name, ironically enough, was Parris French.

"I'm beginning to dislike this plan more each minute," French said, looking down at the folders spread before him on the table.

"Was there another way?" Diver respected French's opinions, but was confident that his approach had been correct.

"It's just that this fellow Pine is a pretty bright boy, and if he puts two and two together . . ."

"Suppose he does? What will he be able to do?" King interposed. "Besides, Bigger should make things interesting enough for Pine to keep his mind off what's really happening, if things go wrong."

"Well, that's just it." French looked again at Diver and then at King. "If Bigger applies too much pressure to Pine, he may begin to think. If that happens and he comes up with the right answers, he could blow this entire project. He's not a professional, you know."

"Even so," Diver suggested. "Common sense alone should prevent him from doing something stupid, even if he does discover our little game. Boy, will his feelings be hurt if he gets wind of this program."

"To put it mildly." French was frowning in thought.

Diver had worked hard on this plan. They had called Bigger to Washington, ostensibly because of his excellent record of achievement, and asked him to help in the selection of a courier with whom he would work, to recover some intelligence from one of their agents. They were careful to let Bigger discover accidently that the information to be recovered contained the location of several Soviet missile sites in Nam. French was recalled for home leave and Bigger was left in charge of Security at the Embassy. Although the document that was being used as bait was important and the information contained therein hard intelligence of value to the Americans, it was necessary to use something sufficient to ensure that Bigger would be compelled to secure it. The loss of the data was not nearly as important as learning the identity of Bigger's contacts and the route through which they operated.

Diver felt that Deplint, who was an experienced agent, would not be approached for the document because Pine, who was totally inexperienced and unaware of what was going on, would be a much easier target. They were also reasonably sure that Pine would not be hurt. In fact, Diver expected Pine to be escorted, unknown to him, *en route* to the Embassy by Bigger's people, and the papers conveniently delivered to Bigger, who would predictably copy the document, file the original, and transfer the copy to his contact. Pine would then be out of it and a surveillance of Bigger could then be effected; when he made his contact, the tail would report its location and the entire cabal would be short-circuited. Bigger could then be fed as much misinformation as the American authorities desired, and until he was compromised by the misinformation, he would finally be truly working for the Government.

When Bigger reported to Diver, later that day, that Pine had missed his pick-up, Diver could not understand what had gone awry with Deplint. The loss of the intelligence without a return on the investment was crushing. But when they subsequently learned from an American operative in French Intelligence that Soviet agents had searched Pine's hotel room, Diver was encouraged to believe that Bigger had not yet got possession of the document.

A subsequent report that two East Germans who were working for the Russians had been killed at the drop-site had further encouraged Diver to believe that Pine might actually have got the list himself; if Pine had killed these men, and it looked very much as if he were the instrument of their death, it was likely that they had assaulted him in an attempt to get the document from him. Their deaths bespoke their failure. But why they should have disregarded what surely must have been Bigger's instructions could not be explained, unless Bigger's superiors suspected that he had been compromised and had sought other ferrets to secure the data that was so important for them to recover. Also, why Pine did not turn the information over to Bigger, if he had it, was a clinker; did Pine himself suspect Bigger because of something that had happened when he saw the fat man at the Embassy? Leave it to the Marines, Diver reflected.

The interest of French Intelligence in the matter, however, complicated things a bit as did their search of Pine's hotel room, as reported by the planted American agent at the *Deuxième Bureau*. Although the search had disclosed nothing, the later Russian search was still an unknown quantity. Only that Pine had disappeared the following day with the Kennedy girl gave Diver any hope that Pine might still have the document in his possession, if he ever had it. The results of the Soviet raid would not be known until Pine had been located.

The final blow came when Diver got word that the French police were now looking for Pine, in connection with the death of the two Germans. A call to the Paris Embassy found Bigger gone for the weekend; he was also absent from his apartment. They had hoped that pressure on Bigger from the Embassy would keep him from acting against Pine until Diver could fly to Paris. It had been a long day and the project was getting very much out of hand.

Then a report arrived that the French police had been put onto Pine by Bigger himself. Now Diver was sure that Pine had become suspicious of Bigger and that the fat man knew it.

"We've got to get someone over to Paris and find Pine before anyone else does," commented French. "Especially Bigger. If he . . . "

The telephone rang shrilly on a small table behind Diver. He leaned his chair back on two legs and reached for the receiver.

"Okay, and thanks," he replied, scribbling an address on a pad. "It looks as if our boy has turned up." He smiled at the others around the table.

"Dead?" French had a resigned look on his face.

"Far from," Diver remarked. "It appears that he's shacked-up with that little girl he picked up. He's in the apartment of some old school chum of his. The guy and his wife are on vacation in Rome and heard the broadcast of Pine's involvement with the police before they left Paris. He reported to the Rome Embassy as soon as he arrived." Diver's grin had broadened. "And I believe, for the time being at any rate, that we are the only ones who know where he is."

"At a time like this, shacked-up. Sonofabitch!" said King, shaking his head.

If there was one thing Pine hated, it was taking a bath. He was too tall for bathtubs and always felt like an idiot, sitting with his knees bunched up and his testicles floating towards the surface. Besides, he had a feeling that there was something unhygienic about sitting in a few gallons of water, surrounded by one's own dirt. In the States, his frequent showers were his primary method of relaxation, but since having come to France, the accommodations had been in older buildings that had not yet entered the twentieth century. Charlie's apartment had a shower attachment connected to the bath-tub, but it was no fun standing naked in the middle of a rather drafty room unprotected by curtains, holding a sprayer over one's head. The baths would have to do.

Actually, once in it, he found the hot water extremely relaxing and in his present physical condition, the applied heat of the surrounding water was soothing to his battered body. Every few minutes, he would let a little water out of the tub and add some more hot. The longer he stayed in the tub, the less inclined he was to step out. After about forty minutes of luxuriation, he was totally enervated. With wrinkled pink skin, he lifted his frame out of the water and dripped out upon the small bathroom floor mat.

Attempting to restore sensation to his heat-numbed surfaces, he gave himself as vigorous a rubdown as his body could stand, noting that his aches had left him for the time being, at least. Donning a soft flannel shirt and the only pair of slacks that he had brought over with him, Pine slippered his way into the living room. Laura had bathed in the other bathroom and had slipped into a pair of slacks and a short-sleeved sweater. She looked delicious. Having put on some soft music and having made Pine a drink, she was reclining on the couch, leafing through a French fashion magazine.

Pine walked over to her and kissed her lightly on the forehead.

"I'm sorry I got you into this mess, Laura." The strain of the past few days was catching up with him, not to mention jet lag. He could feel the drawn sensation of nervous fatigue pulling at his body.

"I know I should be sorry too, but I'm not." She smiled up at him and kissed one of his hands.

"We've got a lot to discuss this evening, you know. Somehow, we've got to get out of this mess. With the police after us now, we won't be able to move as freely, but at least we've got a safe hideout, I hope," he said, remembering the broadcast and the possibility that Blegg had heard it, too.

Pine took a large swallow of Scotch, and mentally began to choose their options, as Laura prepared dinner.

There were at least two groups looking for them. On one hand, there was Bigger and the Soviets who wanted to kill him. There was, perhaps, another group composed of some undisclosed person or persons who had searched his room at the hotel before the Russians, and although he did not know who they might be, they would have to be put in the same class as Bigger, even if their prior attempt had not indicated murder as a prime motive. And finally, the French police were after him on suspicion of murder. The American authorities would probably join in the search with the police to assuage any damage he might have visited upon Franco-American relations, assuming, of course, that such relations actually existed.

Of course, Bigger, through his offices, would most likely have access to any information secured by both the police and, if the Americans did assist, to their efforts as well. This meant that Bigger would likely get to him first; Pine had better be prepared to defend himself.

Another problem was how he would clear himself if the authorities found him, which he was certain they would, given time and assuming, of course, that Bigger did not succeed first. It had been Bigger, no doubt, who had tipped off the police about the murders, and the French police were notorious for their efficiency in crime detection.

There was one saving grace, however, without which Pine might have thrown in the proverbial towel and turned himself in, if for nothing else, for protection. Because of the publicity attendant on the case, Diver or King might get word of the situation. They would know that the charges arose out of the mission on which he had been sent. To protect him, they might intervene. But there was also the possibility that Diver and King were tied in with Bigger, in which case, Pine had really had it. It was, after all, only through Diver, King or Bigger, that he could prove his innocence.

12

Laura began dinner with sardine hors d'oeuvres. After a small portion of fettuccini Alfredo, she served chicken with lemon slices and a large salad, liberally sprinkled with her own vinegar mustard dressing. A cool bottle of Muscadet complemented the meal nicely. Pine would leave a note for Charlie regarding his use of the food and the wine, and a few dollars to cover costs; Charlie's wife might have a nervous breakdown otherwise, and never forgive poor Charlie for giving Pine the key. A few flowery words of praise for the decor would also help soothe the savage breast.

With dinner finished and the dishes all cleared, Pine began to feel his bruises again. The relief produced by the hot bath had gone and the soreness had returned.

"We've got three bedrooms to choose from," Laura said, noticing the stiffness of Pine's motions.

"This middle one looks like a guest room of sorts. Why don't we use it?" Pine suggested.

"You go ahead and get into bed," she said, pulling out the shirt tails of her blouse. "I'll only be a minute or two."

Laura went towards the bathroom, grabbing a few things as she left the room.

Pine undressed slowly, taking care not to rub or bang any of his injured parts. As he looked at his naked body in the full length mirror, he could see a slight swelling around his ribs and a gash on the inside of his right thigh, where the Russian's boot had rasped an open cut. His face was not too bad, except for a puffiness on the outside of the left eye socket. The cut on his arm had already begun to heal and was, in fact, beginning to itch. Other than that, he saw a tall lean form that had not yet started to sag or spread. Despite the events that had precipitated his present dilemma, he had a general feeling of well-being, perhaps in part, as the result of too much wine.

The sheets were silk. Sliding between them, he braced himself against their coldness and lay back to await Laura. The bed was king-sized, and Pine stretched his body as far as he could, enjoying the soft uncramped support of a good mattress. The only problem was the sheets, which had already begun to slide off his body. Silk sheets were a pain in the butt, he reflected, resting his head back and closing his eyes for a moment.

When Laura returned to the room wearing bikini panties and matching French bra, Pine was lying on his back, eyes closed, a complaisant smile on his face. He was fast asleep. For a moment she pondered wakening him, but decided that he needed the sleep and she needed time to think. Slipping under the covers next to him, she could feel his hard body against her softness. She had not lied to him when she had said that someone was waiting for her in New York, but she had not been entirely truthful in implying that she was waiting with equal anticipation.

Lying beside Pine, she felt the same curious sense of security that she had felt earlier with him, and which she had never felt with any other man. Under the circumstances, it was ridiculous to feel secure. Laura lay back and watched Pine as he slept peacefully. The sheets were constantly drifting off the bed, and as she let them fall, she could see the body that was arousing in her once again that great desire she had felt the night before at the hotel.

Laura reached across Pine's chest and gently entwined her fingers in the hair on his chest. Pulling herself closer to him, she kissed him lightly on the edge of his mouth, and ran her hand down to his belly. Again she kissed him, not trying to awaken him, enjoying the sensation of seduction as if the man were a mannequin and she were free to exercise her wildest fantasies upon him.

As she ran her hand lower, she noticed that he was responding to her touch and he murmured in his sleep as she continued to excite him. Moving her body against his, she kissed him on the breast, her hair falling over his face, her excitement complete. As if by silent signal, his eyes drifted open, but he lay there without moving, breathing in the fragrance that she exuded, enjoying the delicate contact that she made.

Slowly, she raised her lips to his and he grabbed her to himself. If their first experience had been unexpected and rather awkward as a result of the chilled room and the inadequate facilities, their lovemaking now was deliberate and with the freedom of total release. The sensuous bed sheet beneath them fueled their bodies with additional passion, and the false security that the clandestine apartment lent to the past evening created an abandon that fired their emotions. Despite the fatigue that he felt, Pine acted renewed; Laura's reactions were so fully uninhibited that any prior recognition by her of such a capacity would have been embarrassing.

After the first uncontrollable surge of motion had been slaked, and they had resolved themselves into a quiet, gentle retouching, they began to speak and to exchange tender words. Pine held her face in caring hands and lightly kissed her eyes, and the tears that had been awakened from them rolled in a single path down her cheek and onto the silken bedcover. As his lips worked down her body, she could feel the need again building within her and the urgency grabbed at her chest and at her deepest soul.

Their second lovemaking that evening was slower and more enduring. Pine, who began to weaken as time and effort drew away his remaining energies, was content at first to seek only her gratification; and the duration of his attentions was to him as peaceful as the sleep from which he had been drawn. But as more time and effort were spent, he discovered within himself a new force that passion concentrated into a moment of ultimate exertion, leaving both of them gasping in fulfillment and depletion.

They lay beside each other afterwards, watching eyes, touching hair, saying nothing. Pine's eyes kept dropping and Laura waited until once again he drifted into sleep. Once more she kissed him, and then allowed herself to lie back and relive the experience, an occasional tear still falling from the corner of her eye. She fell asleep with a leg curled around him.

Pine awoke at five-thirty in the morning and found Laura snuggled into the crook of his arm; his arm had fallen asleep. He had slept about eight hours, but still felt drugged and tired. Smiling at the sleeping Laura, he disengaged himself and turned over to sleep for another hour or so. As he moved, Laura stirred, and after saying his name in sleep, fell back into a more restful position. Pine wondered, without really worrying, who the man in New York could be. Before he could ponder the question for long,however, he drifted back into a deep dreamless sleep.

When Pine reawakened, he felt better. His eyes were not crusty and his body seemed to have recovered some during his long rest. Glancing at his watch, he saw that it was quarter to eight. Laura was sitting in a small arm chair next to the bed, watching him speculatively. She appeared to have been up for a while and looked washed and combed. Pine smiled at her.

"Why don't you come and join me? It's nice and warm in here," he said.

Reaching for a glass of tomato juice that she had placed on the night table earlier, she came to the bed, handed Pine the glass, and sat down. Pine drank the juice and then looked up at her with mock lechery.

Pulling her to him, he kissed her strongly. Laura slid under the covers with him and placed her arms lightly about his neck, drawing her body against his when the door bell sounded. At first, Pine ignored the door, but the caller continued to ring furiously.

"Who the hell could that be?" His brows wrinkled in concentration. "I'm sure Charlie's friends all know that he's gone. It may be trouble, Laura."

"I'll give them trouble, those bastards."

Pine rose from the bed and pulled on a pair of trousers. Grabbing a letter opener with a long firm blade from the bedroom desk, he told Laura to keep hidden and went to the door; he held the blade behind his back. If it were Bigger, he decided that he would attack first and ask questions never; if it were the police, he decided to give up quietly. It was Diver and King. Pine did not know what to do.

"Sorry to waken you, Pine, but we heard you'd got yourself into a bit of a mess," Diver said with a grin.

"And whom have I to thank for that?" Pine answered, not

yet sure of either of the two after his experience with Bigger.

"Well, aren't you going to invite us in? Where's your hospitality?" King was in a good mood; Pine was not.

"What happened with Bigger?" Diver asked. "He reported to us that you hadn't made the pick-up."

"I'll just bet he did. Why don't you ask Bigger?" Pine brought the letter opener to his side, hanging limply in his hand. "After all, he's your boy, isn't he?"

Diver and King glanced at each other for a moment.

"What exactly do you know about Bigger?" King asked, looking at the blade that Pine was now using to scratch at a spot on his neck. "You don't have to worry, you know," he said with a smile. "You can put the knife down."

Diver opened his jacket, displaying a small gun in a shoulder holster.

"Take it if you don't trust us. Go ahead."

Pine took it. Checking to see if the little Beretta was loaded, Pine went into the living room with the others and placed the letter opener on a table; he held the gun in his lap. Feeling better with a real weapon at his disposal, he sat down on the couch opposite the two men who had taken chairs. Laura came into the room and joined Pine on the couch; he introduced her to the two Americans.

"Whether you know it or not, Bigger tried to get me killed. And more than once, too. I'm sure it was Bigger."

"What makes you so sure it was him?" asked Diver.

Pine told them everything that had happened since his arrival in Paris. He carefully went over his conclusions and summed up with an explanation of his present situation, as he saw it. King and Diver glanced at one another a few times during the discourse. When Pine had finished, Diver rose and walked to the curtained window; he peered into the street and said nothing for a long time. After a while, he said:

"You've stated the problem nicely. Now, how to you propose to get out of it?"

"Why you sonofabitch!" Pine exploded, rising from his seat. "How do *I* expect to get out of it? You got me into this mess and I think you had better get me the hell out of it.

"Look, I didn't know what this was about when I got into it," Pine continued more calmly. "And you guys weren't too careful to fill me in. Now I want to know what *you* intend to do."

"You were well-paid for it, Pine," King said sympathetically.

"Well-paid, my ass," cried Pine. "Five grand is not what I consider well-paid to get my brains beat out and before this is over, I may even be killed."

"Well, look Pine." Diver had turned from the window and was facing into the room now. "We'll help you out of this thing, but you've got to help us, too. From what you remember of the list, you can see that it's important we get the information back. It's also important that we clear up the matter of Bigger."

"I don't know," Pine remarked sullenly. "What exactly do you want me to do? Then I'll tell you. But this time, my friend, you had better let me in on the whole story, because if I find out later that I've been had again, you fellows might just . . . "

"Okay, okay!" King interrupted. "How about putting up some coffee?" he said to Laura.

Diver outlined the plan that had been devised to entrap Bigger; he assured the agitated man that they had not expected him to have such a large role in the project. He explained how suspicion of Bigger had developed when one of the Washington Security guards had recognized him. The guard had, at one time, been with the Chicago police, and had remembered Bigger from the days when he had run a vice organization in the thirties.

But the plan had not succeeded. Apparently Bigger's contact had instructed the two men who assaulted Pine at the drop to stop him and take the intelligence so that Bigger would not get it. If Bigger's own people felt that he had been compromised, the only recourse now was to clean up as much of the opposition team as they could. And that meant getting Bigger.

King said that the only way to snare Bigger now was to let him find Pine. Bigger was sure to realize that his days at the Embassy were over if Pine got to the American authorities before Bigger could stop him, despite the lack of hard proof; the questions that would be raised by their conflicting stories would suffice. The only solution for Bigger was to kill Pine and be done with it. The more he heard, the less Pine liked the plan.

"You said something before about French Intelligence being interested in me as well," Pine commented. "Aside from the police, how do they fit into it?"

Diver looked at Laura.

"You might as well tell us," Pine interjected. "She's been in this with me from the beginning. Besides, whom is she going to tell?"

"Well, actually," King began. "We suspect that the French have been involved with the Russians in Nam. In fact, one of the reasons France has been so cozy with the Russians lately is that they have a common economic interest. You realize that France gets a great deal of her rubber from plantations in North Viet Nam.

"Of course, France will get the short end of the rod from the Soviets; I don't understand why they can't see that. Russia's just using France for her purposes; she would never trust a nation as unstable as the French Republic with her close ties to the West."

Pine still did not see why France should be interested in him.

"Well, don't you see?" Diver added. "Although France is working with Russia in Nam, Russia is not going to open its doors and give the French such things as their guidance systems or their nuclear warhead technology. France figures that if she could obtain some of this weaponry, it would give her greater bargaining power with us as well as with the Russians. You know how she is trying to establish her own nuclear technology?

"If France knew where the Soviet missile sites were located, they might . . . well . . . we don't know exactly what they might do, but it could get messy. The point is that we don't want France to get this intelligence any more than we want the Russians to retrieve it."

"What about Miss Kennedy?"

"We'll take care of her," Diver answered. "No harm will come to her."

"You realize that the police are after her, too?" Pine added.

"We'll have no trouble clearing it with local police authorities after this blows over. Until then, we'll keep her safe, I assure you; then charges will be dropped against both of you." Diver seemed quite certain. Pine felt that Diver and King had done this kind of thing before; he did not know, however, if they had been successful; it bothered him more than he wanted to admit.

But he was greatly relieved to have Diver and King take over the planning of the operation. It was also comforting to know that the things he had done, and the things he expected he might have to do again, had the sanction of authority, particularly when the authority had final jurisdiction over him.

13

Bigger had not seriously begun to worry. He needed only to get to Pine before he got to the American authorities. He knew that it would be more difficult to restore his credibility with Moscow, but after dealing with Pine, he would deal with that problem.

As he left the Embassy, walking through Place de la Concorde and up the Champs, Bigger began to consider methods to locate his target. He knew that Pine, as an amateur, would not have contacts enabling him to hide for long; the police would soon find him. When that occurred, he would demand to see Pine immediately. Of course, were he to find Pine first, it would eliminate the difficult problem of how to kill him while he was in police custody.

Bigger had already checked with his agent at the Prefecture and had learned that the cab that Pine had taken in the Latin

Quarter was a dead-end; the Turkish bath to which Pine had gone disclosed nothing that could lead to his capture. At present, all cabs in Paris were being checked by the police to determine if any of them had picked him up later. The hotels would be investigated that evening, after the new cards had been deposited with the police, and Bigger would know the results of these investigations as soon as the police did themselves.

Continuing past the Étoile, Bigger turned left and proceeded toward his apartment building. As he approached the front of the structure, a black Bentley with liveried chauffeur pulled up to his side, the back door opening ominously. Seated inside were two men, one of whom was dressed in a dark twill, single-breasted suit with the square cut style peculiar to the Eastern European. The other man was wearing black slacks and a black turtle neck sweater. The suited man instructed him to enter the car; Bigger began to perspire.

Neither man spoke after Bigger was in the car. Blinds that covered the passenger windows were tightly drawn, and without a word of instruction, the driver pulled away from the curb and on his course. Bigger sat on a small uncomfortable seat that faced the rear of the car so that he was forced to face the two men who sat opposite him.

Despite his ruthless appearance, the suited man could easily have been any businessman en route to a Board of Director's meeting. The other man, however, was an entirely different story.

He was tall and straight. His mouth curved down with a natural scowl that made him look as if were perpetually angry. Across the right side of his face, which was not unhandsome, ran a scar from the lobe of his ear to the corner of his mouth. It was not deep, but it was definite; it did nothing to soften his appearance. His hands were huge and heavily scarred. There

113

was no question in Bigger's mind that this man was a professional killer of the highest competency.

"Where are we going?

"Look here," Bigger demanded. "You can't treat me like this. I have powerful connections; I'm an important man; I'm..."

"Shut up!" the suited man said dangerously. The other remained silent, his expression unchanged.

Sitting silently, uneasy at his prospects, Bigger could feel the car expertly guided through the Paris afternoon traffic. From the lessening noise, they appeared to be headed towards the suburbs. After about an hour, the Bentley turned right and its pace slackened to a slow crawl. The condition of the road was poor and after about five more minutes on the bad road, the driver turned left and pulled up on a smooth stretch that ran for about one minute. The car stopped and the driver cut the ignition.

Bigger was helped out of the car and was led to a large chateau. The men led Bigger through the large foyer and stopped before a massive door. The suited man rapped gently and a voice responded in Russian. The door was opened, Bigger was nudged into the room, and the door closed behind him.

The room was large. The entire back wall was an expanse of French doors that looked over a wide and well kept lawn. The central doors opened to a walkway that led through formal gardens towards cabanas and a pool. Bigger could see tennis courts in the distance.

Inside the room, the furniture was luxurious, but quiet. It was done in the browns and reds that denote a man's abode, but there were tasteful touches that bespoke a decorator's hand. Directly in front of and centered on the French doors was a giant walnut desk. In other circumstances, Bigger would have been delighted by the good taste.

The man who sat behind the desk was as unsightly as the room was elegant. He was, perhaps, five-foot-two or three inches tall and could not have weighed more than one hundred ten pounds. On his face were two sunken hollows that pretended to be eyes and a large gaping hole that screamed mouth. His hair, or what was left of it, was a grayish dirty brown, greasy and unkempt. But his hands were immaculate. Each fingernail was neatly trimmed and polished and the hands were big and beautifully shaped. It was the one aspect of this man's physique that shone and it was obvious that he was both aware of it and determined to make the most of it.

"Sit down, Bigger," he said in a strong, deep voice.

"My name is Shaskof!" he said. "I am not too happy with your failure to carry out your assignment. I have you to thank for being sent to this pitiful country, and it is my job now to determine why a certain American, who has seen documents that are rather sensitive, is still alive. What troubles me even more is why you have not been able to retrieve the document itself, which I understand was practically placed into your hands." Shaskof paused and stared directly into Bigger's watery eyes.

"I have, er, put into operation the necessary, that is, the steps are being . . . " Bigger had heard of Shaskof and knew that he was a troubleshooter for the KGB, summoned only in cases where they were considering the termination of an agent in charge of an operation who had failed and who remained an embarrassment. He had full authority to use anything or to do anything that came into his mind, and his mind and his methods were famously unpleasant.

"You are a dead man, Bigger," Shaskof said softly. "I do not envy the manner in which you will die." There was a touch of sympathy in his voice, but it did not ring quite true. "You have performed service to the Soviet Republic in the past, but this

115

blunder of yours has reduced your previous adequacy to worthlessness." Shaskof took a small automatic pistol from the desk drawer and laid it gently on the walnut desktop before him.

"But it is more important that the American be stopped than revenge be taken against you," Shaskof continued. "So!" he paused dramatically. "We will give you until Monday evening at eighteen hundred hours to destroy this Pine. If you succeed, we will consider your mission a success *in toto*—and you will be allowed to continue your useless existence. In fact, since it may be necessary for you to compromise your position in the West, in order to hit the American, we will even provide you with safe passage to the Soviet Union and an insignificant job upon which you will be able to sustain yourself.

"But if you fail, your fate will make Dante's *Inferno* seem pleasurable," Shaskof laughed, shoving the automatic over the desk to Bigger.

"If you do not use it on the American," Shaskof continued, after the gun was in Bigger's hand, "perhaps it would be wise to use it on yourself. That is all." Bigger stumbled from the room numbly, stuffing the firearm into his jacket pocket. He knew that Shaskof meant every word that he had said.

Back in the room, Shaskof poured a shotglass of vodka for himself and for the man who had entered from a side door when Bigger had left.

"Well, Boris," he said jovially. "What do you think? Will our fat friend succeed?"

"I do not know for sure, Comrade. Bigger can be an efficient agent, but this time I think he has got himself in too deep. It is almost certain that his cover is blown; he is no longer a safe risk."

"Exactly, my friend." Shaskof swallowed the shot of vodka in one gulp and poured himself another; Boris's glass stood empty, but was not refilled.

Bigger arrived back in Paris at about seven-thirty that Friday evening. After being driven back to his apartment by the chauffeur, he picked up an alternate passport, drafted in the name of Thurston Woodbury Harrison III, and packed a small overnight bag. Catching a cab at a corner near the Étoile, he directed the driver to the Hotel Bristol and sat back to ponder his approach to Pine. Bigger was confident that he would get him, but not about what it would cost him to do it. Pine would pay for the anguish he had gone through with Shaskof. Pine would pay in blood.

14

Diver and King escorted Pine and Laura from the building in Avenue Mozart and to an unmarked Embassy car parked on the opposite side of the street. It was decided that they would be relocated in a hotel where rooms had been taken in Diver's and King's names so that they would not have to use their own passports. Laura would be left at the hotel and Pine would accompany Diver and King in pursuit of their objective. It was eleven-thirty in the morning.

Driving back into the center of Paris, the car entered Rue Fauberg St. Honore and drove up the street to number 112. The small distinguished awning quietly proclaimed the Hotel Bristol. A dignified doorman ushered them in and they descended the few steps to the small unpretentious reception desk, facing the main entrance. Turning to the left, the party walked to the main lobby and then immediately to the right, where an antique elevator took them to the fourth floor. The two suites adjoined, one registered in Diver's name, the other in King's. Stepping into Diver's rooms, they went into a small parlor where they all took seats.

"Not bad for a public servant," Pine remarked, looking around in appreciation.

"We have a reasonable allowance at times," King replied, "but not for ourselves, unfortunately. We're better off here, though, because we'll get the least questions asked and the most privacy. This suite is yours, Pine. The one next door is for Miss Kennedy. I'm afraid that Diver and I will have to head back to our own cold water flat later."

"For the time being, Miss Kennedy," Diver suggested, as he picked up the telephone and dialed for an outside line, "it would be best if you remained in until we return. If you want anything, call room service and don't use your correct name. We shouldn't be more than a few hours."

The party he had phoned did not answer and Diver replaced the receiver, rose and motioned the other men to follow him towards the door.

"Be careful. Please?" Laura said, as they left.

With Diver and King present, Pine felt considerably more secure. While Laura had been with them, he had felt a tension that resulted in part from his growing affection for her and in part from the concern that she was exposed to constant danger.

"What exactly are you, er, I mean, we, looking for?" Pine asked.

"Actually, we don't know yet. We're going to Bigger's apartment now; he wasn't in when I called back at the Bristol. Maybe he left something lying about the apartment that will give us a clue as to how to spring our little trap," King replied.

"And I'm the bait, I suppose." Pine said.

King directed the driver to stop a block or so away from the apartment; the three men walked the rest of the way. They entered the building and took the stairs to the third floor, and after knocking tentatively to assure that no one was there, Diver removed a thin leather wallet from his pocket. He proceeded to flick through long, narrow, metal tools that were neatly contained within. Selecting the instrument that he wanted, he inserted it into the lock and turned once. The lock snapped open instantly and they entered the room. Pine looked back at the door and then at the pouch that Diver was replacing in his inside pocket.

"Pretty neat little trick. Where can a guy get hold of a kit like that?"

"Any hood in New York can make one for you," King admitted. "An expert with a well-made set of these tools can open almost any keylock within a few seconds."

"Boy! What a set-up," Pine commented. "How much are we paying you guys these days?"

"It's funny, you know," King remarked. "If it weren't for Bigger's penchant for high living, we might not have caught on to him so easily. It's not customary, needless to say, for a minor Embassy officer to wear three-hundred dollar suits and to eat and live in the kind of places that Bigger frequents, unless, of course, he has another source of income. It was the other source of income that began to bother us."

They looked briefly through the other rooms before beginning their search in earnest. Diver and King worked fast and had planned to make a shambles of the rooms before they finished, and they were going to leave behind something of Pine's. Although Bigger had enough reason to seek Pine out, they wanted to include a little personal pressure to spur his incentive.

The article they had decided to leave was his wallet, containing the receipt from the Candide and another receipt from a small private hotel in the Latin Quarter. A stake-out at the little hotel would be posted as soon as they had left Bigger's apartment. Two hundred dollars in francs and American currency were placed in the wallet, together with assorted business cards and papers.

The room disclosed nothing. Bigger was a professional, and had not left incriminating evidence behind. The wallet was left near the foot of a couch that had been overturned. When they left the apartment, it needed redecoration.

Shaskof was having a manicure. Boris sat at a small table at the other end of the room, looking through the wide French doors. Although nothing had been said, it was understood that any failure by Bigger reflected indirectly upon him; he was Bigger's contact and his superior.

Looking out over the lawn, he could see Yori down by the pool. The water was littered with leaves and had not yet been emptied for winter. Yori, quiet and strange, was seated by the edge of the pool, watching the water as he often did. At times, the household employees would find small animals and birds that had drowned.

Boris did not know a great deal about Yori, although he knew that he never slept with women and did not have inclinations towards men. However, Yori got some deep sexual satisfaction from killing and especially from torturing a victim. Perhaps it was this that scared him most, for he knew that someday, Yori might be ordered to work on him. When that day came, Boris resolved that he would be dead before Yori got within ten feet of him.

Boris's reflections were interrupted by the burr of the telephone. Shaskof, careful not to smear his nail polish, lifted up the receiver between thumb and second finger. Speaking for a moment in monosyllabic grunts, and glancing once at Boris, he slowly straightened in his chair and pushed a button on the side of the desk. Before he had replaced the receiver, a servant had entered the room and stood at attention near the door. Shaskof instructed him to get Yori and turned to Boris.

"Bigger's apartment has just been searched by Pine and two others," he said grimly. "One of the others was recognized to be a man named Diver who is with American Intelligence."

Boris stiffened in his seat.

"It seems that Pine was able to make contact with his people, notwithstanding the French Police, the French Secret Service, and our own efforts.

"Now," he continued, "we've got to rectify these defects in our security. Bigger must not be apprehended by the Americans; he knows too much about our operations and, of course, he has seen me here as well as having been to this chateau. He has become dangerous. He must be terminated."

Shaskof looked up as Yori walked into the room and stood silently next to the door fingering the long scar that ran along the right side of his face.

"Yori," Shaskof said. "You remember the fat man you brought here yesterday?"

Yori nodded his head, his eyes cold.

"Well," Shaskof smiled. "He has become an embarrassment."

"Yes, Comrade."

"Don't waste too much time on him, Yori." Boris was not sure, but he thought that a slight look of disappointment passed over the cold eyes. "I want you to return as quickly as possible. There may be more work for you later."

Shaskof told him to wait in the car for Boris, and Yori stepped quietly out of the room.

"Now comes the real problem, Boris." Shaskof picked up a pencil, starting to doodle on a pad that lay before him.

"Pine's got to be stopped. He's seen our intelligence and, perhaps, has passed its contents on to his friends. If so, there is little we can do about that, but he must be stopped. We do not know what else he may have learned about us through Bigger. We don't even know how he found out about Bigger. If we had more time, we could have him brought here and questioned, because I now suspect that he is not really the amateur they pretend, but a new fieldman whom we've not met before.

"As far as Diver and the other American are concerned, we'll have to stop them, too. But I leave the details to you, Boris. Don't fail me.

"Get going now, and send Yori back as soon as you've done with him. You'll remain in Paris until you've completed the entire mission. I wish you good luck."

Boris left the room and walked across the wide entrance hall towards the front door. He was not sure where to begin his search but decided to start at Bigger's apartment. His first concern was to get Bigger, which he felt should not take more than a few hours. He knew all his haunts and hideouts and was even aware that he had a false passport in the name of Harrison; he was sure Bigger did not know that the Harrison identity had also been blown. After a quick look around the apartment, he would contact his own people in Paris to see if either the name Bigger or Harrison had appeared on the hotel registration cards filed the previous evening with the police. Meanwhile, he would send out his ferrets. These specialists had served him well in the past and although they tended to be expensive, now was not the time to worry about his operational costs. Besides, Bigger would pay for the expense.

During the search, he would wait at Bigger's place, as it was unlikely that the Americans would return there. Of course, if they did, it would simplify his job considerably, especially since Yori would be with him. And then again, Bigger himself, might return. After he dealt with him, he would let word out to locate Diver, who would lead him to Pine and the other one; they would be easy to dispose of. His only problem was that it be done quickly. Entering the car, he turned to Yori who was sitting in the farthest corner at the back of the vehicle, looking straight ahead, without a sign of emotion or of tension on his face.

"Is everything ready, Yori?"

"Yes."

Boris drove down the long driveway, along the dirt road, and into the main highway. Keeping his speed just under the legal limit, he drove directly back to Paris and parked the car a few blocks from Bigger's apartment building. He and Yori walked unrushed into the main entrance and using the stairs, ascended to his rooms.

The door was opened without difficulty and Boris observed the condition of the apartment. Boris liked to see a job well done, and could not help admiring the thoroughness of the Americans. He knew that their execution would have to be effected without preamble and with dispatch; they would take advantage of any delay or error that he might make. Looking over the apartment, he was sure that nothing of importance had been missed. He did not expect that Bigger had left much to be found, but he had already made one too many mistakes and could have made another.

Suddenly he heard a rattle in the doorlock. The two men slipped quietly into the small bedroom, and Boris partially closed the door behind them.

15

After he had checked into the Bristol, Bigger began planning his attack. He knew that Pine was on his own, except, of course, for the Kennedy woman whom he expected would be more of a hindrance than a help. He figured that Pine would hesitate to approach the authorities at least for several days. He would doubt their trustworthiness after his experiences with Bigger, not to mention the police manhunt that faced him.

After a large dinner, Bigger walked to a corner café where he could purchase telephone tokens. From the rear of the café Bigger phoned half a dozen operatives whose help he needed. They would check all the hotels and private rooming houses. Although he imagined that Pine would not be so foolish as to register in a hotel where he could be traced through registration cards, he hoped that under pressure he had been careless and used a public facility. It was fortunate that a passport was required to register in any Parisian rooming facility.

His next step was to arrange for various members of his personal underworld to stake-out certain public places where a man might spend an evening or, perhaps, a night. Each of these had Pine's description. The agents were instructed to leave word at the Mail Desk of the Paris Ritz for a Monsieur Martin Blaine. Returning to the Bristol, Bigger retired for the night. In the morning, after checking at the Ritz, he would begin his own personal search.

As he lay in bed that evening, Bigger reflected upon his present situation. He was still not sure how Pine had come to suspect him, although he supposed that Pine must have seen him with the two Germans at the drop in Rue de Vaugirard; he knew that after he had left, neither Hans nor Otto would have spoken, even under threat of death—it was not their style. But he was not sure that Pine had seen him with them. If Pine had found out about him from other sources, the question was when and from whom.

Bigger did not think that Washington had cracked his case yet. But it no longer mattered whether Pine or the American authorities had blown him. Bigger was through being useful to the Russians. Washington would never bust him, but rather would use him themselves as a channel for misinformation.

Bigger, however, had no intention of letting himself be shipped off to some obscure position in Moscow. He knew that the Russians would execute him summarily if they even suspected that he were a danger to them. The American authorities might be less prone to violence, but his future with them was no less dire.

The Chinese, however, might have use of someone who was clever and who came gift-wrapped with valuable intelligence from both Soviet and American sources. And this was exactly what Bigger had been anticipating when, several years ago, he had begun to accumulate information respecting military sites and installations, and espionage teams and organizations, with particular emphasis on those working within the Chinese sphere of influence.

After having returned from his meeting with Shaskof, Bigger had been tempted to make his escape immediately, as he knew that Moscow would dispose of him whether he hit Pine or not; it merely extended his life to pursue Pine for them now. Unfortunately, the banks had all been closed when Bigger had returned to Paris, and he was, therefore, unable to get the money he needed for his exodus, or the documents that would give him welcome passage. He would have to wait until Monday morning, and until then, he had better stay operative since he was sure that he could never hide from either Boris or Shaskof for even one weekend; if it looked as though he were accepting their statements at face value, he would at least live until Monday. Weighing the aspects for his future, Bigger fell into a restless sleep.

Early the next morning, Bigger went to the Paris Ritz to collect such messages as might have come in during the night. Each of his contacts had reported that their bloc had neither found Pine nor had word of him. Annoyed at the failure of his subordinates and the growing danger to himself as a result, Bigger returned to conduct his activities from the Bristol.

Before returning to the Bristol, however, he stopped at the Embassy to collect a few personal items that were of value to him and that he wanted to take with him on his travels East. But upon arriving, he was informed that French had returned to Paris. Greatly disturbed, Bigger quickly took his leave, uncertain of the meaning of this unexpected new development.

Bigger waited for the clerk at the reception desk. He was

hoping to arrange for an open line from his room so that he could make outside calls without going through the switchboard. Time was getting short; it was already past noon.

"*Oui, oui Ma'amselle,*" the clerk finished. "That is one sandwich of ham and a pot of coffee. Oh, *mais non, Ma'amselle.* It is not necessary. It will be put on the bill of Monsieur Diver as he has directed."

Bigger almost cried out in surprise. He had not been listening carefully to the conversation, but he had heard the name Diver quite clearly. Was it possible that he also had come to Paris? Was it the same Diver? What was he doing at a hotel such as this? The clerk was peering at Bigger with respectful impatience.

"Yes, Monsieur Harrison," he queried. "May I help you?"

"I just passed by to see if there were any messages while I was out."

The clerk leafed through several individual sheets on the side of the desk and returned his gaze to Bigger.

"I am sorry, Monsieur. Were you expecting someone? I can have the call transferred if you will be out of the hotel later."

"No, no," Bigger replied with a good-natured smile, "that won't be necessary." Bigger turned to leave the desk, hesitated, then turned back to the clerk who had already gone back to his work.

"By the way," he began tentatively. "I heard you say the name Diver on the phone a moment ago. I used to attend school with a man named Diver, er, Percival Diver, if I remember correctly. It couldn't be the same man, I suppose?"

"Why, it is strange, but this gentleman, his name too it is Percival Diver. He is with a Monsieur King. Do you know him too?"

"No. I don't think so. Well, I'm sure it couldn't be the same man."

"Well, if you wish to ring him up, Monsieur, he is in room

406, and Monsieur King is in 408. Even if he is not the same man, he may be amused that you knew someone with the same name, no?"

"Well, perhaps later," he added. "Do you know when he will be back?"

"I could not say, Monsieur," the clerk added politely. "He left early this morning with his friend and another man whom I did not know."

Here was the chance to get directly at the one person who might know where Pine was hiding. And the third man was probably French. He was now relatively certain that they were on to him, but Bigger no longer cared. He would invite himself into the rooms and await Diver's return. The girl was probably a secretary and if necessary, he would kill her and have the room to himself. He realized that he would have to kill both Diver and King, now that they were in Paris, because they would definitely be in the way; killing French, if he was with them, would be a pleasure, as he had never really liked the man. But one thing was certain; before Diver and King were eliminated, they would tell him where to find Pine.

Bigger returned to his rooms to get his revolver and a silencer, and then went down the stairway to room number 406. After listening for a moment, Bigger knocked. A female voice responded "Qui est là?" and Bigger replied "Service." The door opened.

"Yes?" Laura had the feeling that she had met this fat man before, but she could not remember where.

"Excuse me, Miss," Bigger began amiably. "I'm from the Embassy and I have an important message for Mr. Diver. May I come in?" Bigger had recognized Laura almost immediately and hoped that she would not recognize him.

"Well, er, he's not here right now." Laura replied. "Perhaps you could come back later?"

"Nooo. That would not be advisable." Bigger sounded as

129

though he had contemplated the idea for a moment, and then reflecting that the message was too important to chance missing Diver a second time, had rejected it. With a slight hesitation, Laura let the big man into the suite and motioned to a chair.

"I thought you had said 'Service' when I asked who was there."

"Huh, oh yes. I did. I said Embassy Service." He smiled ominously. "I did not get your name, Miss . . ."

"Oh, I'm sorry. I'm Anne Baxter."

"The same as the movie actress?"

"Yes." Laura suddenly remembered where she had seen this man before, recalling the incident at Rue de Vaugirard and his request to search her room. This was Bigger. She hoped that he had not recognized her. Trying to control her panic, Laura prayed that the waiter would soon arrive. Almost as if she had caused him to materialize, a tap sounded at the door. Bigger was looking directly at her and was smiling. She restrained a shudder.

"My French might not be as good as yours, Miss Kennedy, but it is fluent enough. Don't try anything cute with the waiter." He was pointing a large gun at her, keeping it low in the chair so that it was not obvious.

Scared speechless, Laura opened the door and let the waiter wheel in the small tray with the lunch tastefully laid out on top, covered with dish covers and white linen. When the waiter had left, Bigger pointed to the lunch with his pistol.

"I think you had better leave that, Miss Kennedy. We won't have time for you to eat it."

"What are you going to do?" She knew that he would not turn her over to the police. She was also certain that his only interest in her was to get to Pine. When her usefulness was over, he would kill her.

Bigger got up from the chair, walked to the door and

opened it slowly, searching the hall for traffic. He motioned the girl into the hall and tossed her coat to her, placing the pistol in his jacket pocket where, together with his hand, it made an ugly bulge.

"Please don't do anything stupid. I have a silencer on this gun and before anyone knew that you were dead, I would be away. If you are a good girl, there's no reason why you shouldn't walk away from this adventure later this afternoon. Not to worry." Now Laura was sure she was going to die, and soon.

Bigger nudged Laura into the street. He had not bargained for a catch such as this, so early in the day. The girl would know where Pine was, and when he was finished with her, he might even let her go; she could do him little harm. Bigger felt magnanimous. His first step was to get her to a safe place.

16

After leaving Bigger's apartment, Diver telephoned an operations officer and informed him that the bogus hotel receipt had been planted. Pine wanted to call Laura at the same time, but he was rushed into a car that was to take him to the Left Bank hotel, where their operation was to continue.

"What are you worried about?" Diver wanted to know. "She's all right. Besides," he continued, "we'll be back at the hotel before long anyway."

Diver planned to leave Pine at the new hotel and to post a small army of men both on the street and throughout the building; they expected action by day's end. Meanwhile, Diver and King would return to the Bristol, to proceed indipendently. It bothered Pine that they would not reveal what they intended to do, explaining that "if something goes wrong" what he did not know he could not tell. The entire business seemed rather haphazard. He noticed more than once that whenever Diver or King referred to an aspect of the operation that was safe or comfortable, it was "we" who was going to execute it; if there was a trace of danger to be encountered, it was "you" who was the patsy.

Driving down a dark, narrow street behind a book store on the Boul' Mich, the car came to a stop in front of a small, dirty faced building with an old faded sign reading *Hotel de Chance*.

It was not necessary for Pine to sign any registration card, for, it appeared, the hotel was occasionally employed by those not eager to patronize the more conventional residential accomodations that were available.

Pine was escorted to a room on the third floor, which was as shabby as the rest of the building.

"If they don't come for you by midnight, it will probably be too late for today," Diver said. "We'll come back then, so you won't have to sleep here, at least."

"I don't see the purpose of my staying here in the first place. If I'm only to stay until midnight, why should I stay at all. They could come at any time, day or night."

"As a matter of fact," King began with a smile to take some sting from his answer, "there's no real reason for you to stay here, except to keep out of our hair. And there will be less danger, regardless what you may think. With you here, we don't have to worry about your safety and we can do our jobs."

Pine realized that they could have easily placed him in a room at the Embassy, where he would have been completely safe, and the false trail would still lead Bigger to the little hotel. He expressed his constenation, and Diver, looking at King, placed a hand on Pine's shoulder.

"Look," he said. "It's true. We certainly could have done that. But Bigger's not an amateur. He will surely check to see if you actually are in the hotel before he comes to get you. And we are sure that it will be Bigger who comes, because he will be under pressure to kill you; it would be stupid for him to trust someone else to do it for him. Besides, we've given him a personal reason to come after you now. We know his psychological profile rather well. His personal possessions are sacrosanct to him and your destruction of them will outrage him more than any official orders could.

"Our people will be well-hidden, except for one man who will be in the lobby of the hotel here. His excuse is obvious; you'll note the paint and equipment he's carrying. You may be bait, but we expect to pull the line before the fish can bite."

As Diver and King started to leave, Pine stopped them once more.

"How about giving me a gun?"

"Don't be silly," Diver replied. "You might strain yourself pulling the trigger."

Afraid to sleep and having nothing else to do, Pine decided to phone Laura. Descending the dark staircase, he passed the toilet that served all residents on the first three floors, located on the landing between the first and second floors. The door was ajar and Pine could see the roof of the shop next door through the tiny window which was besmirched with grime.

In the lobby he confronted the concierge and asked in French if he could use the phone.

"*Un franc, s'il vous plaît, Monsieur*," she sang.

Pine dialed the Bristol after spending over half an hour trying to find the number in the oddly arranged French phone book. The desk clerk informed him that neither room 406 or 408 answered. Pine knew that Diver and King could not have got back so quickly in the heavy midday traffic, but Laura should have been there. He told the clerk that he was the man who had been with Monsieur Diver and Monsieur King that morning, and asked if the clerk had seen the lady who had entered with them leave the hotel.

"Oh yes, Monsieur," he chortled. "She left just a moment ago with a another friend of Monsieur Diver. A Monsieur Harrison, an old school chum, you say, no?"

"An old school chum, you say? What did he look like?"

"Well, he was rather fat," the clerk said. "He is also a guest at this hotel. I can tell you that he wears very beautiful clothing."

"Does Monsieur Diver know about this? Does he know that this Monsieur Harrison is at the hotel?"

"I do not think so, Monsieur. Monsieur Harrison asked me about Monsieur Diver earlier this afternoon. He was surprised to find him at the same hotel. Is that all, Monsieur?"

"Yes, thank you, Monsieur. *Merci.*" The man had been fat and wore beautiful clothing. It must have been Bigger, Pine was certain. He also realized, too late, that he should have left a message for Diver at the hotel and was just about to call back when the hall guard came up to him and asked that he return to his room.

Pine suddenly remembered the bathroom he had seen on the landing and the little window leading out to the roof. He permitted the guard to escort him to the first landing. As he was about to return to the hallway, Pine turned to him.

"Say, you don't mind if I use this for a moment," indicating the small toilet on the landing. "It's been a long day."

The guard nodded and went down the stairs to his post.

Closing and locking the door behind him, Pine started the water running in the tiny sink that was crudely attached to the wall, and went to inspect the window. The roof of the adjoining shop was about a foot below the bottom of the window ledge. By compressing his shoulders tightly, he was sure that he could squeeze through the window and get to the roof. Stepping upon the toilet seat, he surveyed the area outside; there was apparently nobody there to observe him. Hoisting himself up to the ledge, Pine wedged his upper torso into the

135

small opening. He groaned as his battered rib cage jarred against the window frame. By wiggling and straining his body around the ledge, Pine managed to maneuver his body through the little window. As he fell to the roof, he felt how cold it was getting and remembered that his coat was back in the room upstairs. He pulled his suit jacket tightly about him, and wiping off some of the soot and grime that had adhered to the front of the jacket and pants, made a quick survey of his body. The gash on his arm felt as though it may have started to bleed again but other than that, he was fine, if a little cold and sore.

Crawling to the edge of the roof, Pine saw that he was two storeys above the street. The roof was bordered on two sides by the walls of the adjacent buildings and to the rear was the courtyard that he had seen from the window of his room. His only escape was the street. He knew that whoever was watching the front of the hotel would see him if he jumped. Looking carefully over the edge of the roof, his body pressed flat so as not to be seen, Pine observed a trellis-work that was rotten and rickety, but it was the only apparent avenue of escape. He realized that it had better be soon, before the hall guard inside became suspicious of his long absence.

As he speculated, a small truck began to chug up the street in his direction. Recognizing the opportunity, Pine braced himself for the moment when the truck would be between him and the building directly across the street where he expected other observers to be hidden. As the truck passed below him, he scrambled over the edge of the roof, grabbing the top of the trellis, and swung himself over the side. The trellis gave a dying gasp, and, holding for only a moment, wrenched away from the wall. Pine half slid, half jumped down the face of the building, along the trellis. He reached the ground as the trellis crumbled down upon him.

The truck, which was now passing immediately in front of

the hotel and was still fighting its way up the street, had covered the noise of the trellis as it fell. In order to allow a car to pass from the other direction, the truck had pulled over precariously close to the wall of the building across from the hotel and had effectively shielded Pine. The driver of the oncoming car had stared at Pine for a moment, shrugged and then drove on. Pine did not wait for further comment, but took his leave. The only place that he could think of going was back to Bigger's apartment, where he hoped he would find Laura. He wished he had a gun.

17

Bigger had to bring Laura to a place where he could both interrogate her and continue his operations at the same time. He figured that the Russians would not interfere with his pursuit of Pine until they felt that he was going to be ineffective. Despite French and Diver having arrived in Paris, he still felt that his apartment would be the best place to go. He could always use Laura as a hostage if he had to get out in a hurry.

Pushing Laura ahead of himself, Bigger stepped from the elevator in his building. He shoved her gently towards his door and removed the key from his pocket, opening the door. Laura stepped in ahead of him and gaped at what she saw. Bigger moved around her, holding her arm and stopped at the entrance. Pushing her aside roughly, he pushed the door shut with his foot, not bothering to relock it, and walked to the center of the room. It had taken him years to collect some of the treasures that lay shattered at his feet.

Walking slowly over to her, Bigger reached out with his stubby fingers, and in his fury, tightly grabbed Laura's neck, squeezing and pressing against her bobbing throat. In a moment of sheer terror, Laura felt her breath cut off. She tried to call out, to scream, to claw at Bigger's arms, but without effect. Slowly she felt her body weakening.

"That is no way to treat a lady, my friend." Boris was standing at the door to the bedroom.

"You! What are you doing here? Why have you done this to my apartment?"

"This is not my work, Bigger," Boris told him calmly. "It is the work of your capitalist friends who seem to have arrived before me."

"But, why? What have they to gain by this?"

"Perhaps they were searching for something, Bigger?" Boris's remarks were beginning to break through Bigger's anger. His eyes began to fill with fear and his jaw began to tremble.

"Why are you here, Boris?" It had occurred to Bigger, now that his agitation was subsiding, that Boris's visit was uncharacteristic. "What has gone wrong?"

For the first few minutes, Bigger had not seen Yori. Now he saw him standing inside the small bedroom. Bigger's lower lip began to wobble.

"I am here because the Americans were here. They know all about you Bigger. They came to search for something that will implicate us. You know what that means, don't you?" Boris entered the room, inclined his head in a bowing manner at Laura, and helped her remove her coat. Laura stood slightly bent, not yet able to breathe freely.

"We warned you, fat man," Boris continued in a harder voice. "As soon as the Americans were on to you, it was the end."

"But . . . but . . . I have her!" Bigger pointed to Laura with a look of triumph overlaid with fear. "I have captured *her*. The Americans will give us what we want in exchange for her. They are soft, you will see. Please, Boris." His eyes darted from Boris to Yori and back.

"No, Bigger. You will see."

"But you can't kill me now. Let me try. Let me see if they will do as I say."

"Yori!" Boris commanded. "Take him into the other room. We do not want the young lady to see how poorly a man can die."

Laura stood motionless in the corner of the room near the door. Boris went over to her and gently took her hand. In a soft voice he tried to soothe the frightened girl.

"I am very sorry that you had to be here like this. You do not have to worry, Miss . . . Kennedy, I presume. Nothing will happen to you here."

Leading Laura over to the love seat, he righted the piece of furniture and let her down on it. Just then a horrible scream erupted from the bedroom. Laura gasped, and then, turning her head, was sick behind the small couch. Boris, glanced at Laura, then quickly turned back to peer at the closed bedroom door. Another scream shot out at them from the bedroom and then another and another. Laura was lying back, moaning, half in fear, half in disgust. Suddenly, they heard Bigger's voice at the edge of insanity, high and hysterical, babbling in utter horror.

"NO! no! no, no, no, no, no, no . . . not THAT . . . PLEEEEASE!!" His words were cut off by the most horrendously piercing bellow that Boris had ever heard. Laura fainted. For a few moments there were no sounds from the room. Then, suddenly, as if a radio had been turned on, Boris could hear a man sobbing, and then a groaning attempt at the word "No!" After that there was silence.

Boris walked over to Laura and slapped her gently on both cheeks. Slowly she awoke. Looking directly into her eyes, he took her hand in his.

"Are you awake?"

"Yes," Laura answered numbly.

"Now listen to me," he began. "What you have heard is merely a sample of what Yori can do to a man. What he can do to a woman is much worse, believe me. I know who you are and I know that you must know where Pine is. It is necessary for me to find him. If you tell me now, we will all be saved a great deal of unpleasantness. If you do not tell me, I will be forced to bring you back with me to our superiors who are not as gentle as I. They will let Yori have you. It is foolish to resist now, because later, you will surely talk."

Laura bit her lip sharply. Her fear had begun to depart; the threats had the strange affect of restoring her composure. She knew that she did not have the information that this man sought, so she knew that regardless what happened to her, she could not disclose Pine's location. She suddenly realized that she loved him.

"You may not believe this, but I really don't know where he is. I was taken away by that man," she shuddered as she nodded towards the bedroom, "before Mark could get back to me."

Boris was not sure that she was telling the truth; he could not take the chance that it was a well-told lie. He also figured that the girl might love Pine and would lie for him.

He was uncertain about his next step. He did not like having the girl with him because she would slow him down. He could not keep her, but he did not want to send her back to Shaskof alone with Yori. He was not concerned if they killed her, but torture was something that he could not sympathize with. It might be best, he thought, to return to the chateau with the girl, and to use her as a bargaining point. Perhaps she

141

could even be persuaded to give some information that she did not realize she had.

Haste was becoming more important. By now, Diver and that other American had probably had time to sit down with Pine and get all the information that he remembered from the list, if any. Boris hoped that it would not be much. He felt that this mission should be scrapped and that the cell with which Bigger had worked should be terminated.

It was Boris's conviction that nothing was to be gained by vengeance. He felt that the best interests of Moscow could now be served only by discontinuing a project that had failed. If necessary, missile sites could be changed, although that would probably take quite a few months. But he also knew Shaskof, even though he had only worked with him a few times in the past. Shaskof liked revenge; it was one of the reasons that he was so greatly feared. If he caused one of Shaskof's projects to falter, revenge would be swift and the instrumentality would be Yori.

Boris knew that he could never free the girl now, as much as he wanted to. Yori had seen her and would report her presence to Shaskof. If Shaskof thought for a moment that he, Boris, had been holding out on him, or not giving full cooperation, Boris could kiss his dreams of tomorrow good-bye. This woman had to talk.

"You must listen to me, young woman. If you do not believe that you will tell us what we want, I will show you how wrong you are." Taking her by the arm, Boris tugged her to the door of the bedroom in which Bigger had just died.

Laura fought to keep away from the door. She knew that if she saw what was left inside, judging from the screams, she might break. She did not think that she knew anything, but she might know just enough to get Pine killed. They still did not know where Bigger had found her.

Throwing open the door, Boris pushed Laura inside the room. Laura stood to the side of the door and faced the bed, her face a sickly green. Lying spread eagled, stark naked on the bed, was a caricature of a man. The face was contorted and the body was fixed at death in the most gruesome posture. The mouth was wide agape with blood seeping out along the edges. The nose was an unrecognizable smear across the left side of the face. Where the eyes had been were two deep bloody sockets that appeared to be pulsating with a life of their own, still writhing with the agony of their last moments. Laura tried to look away, but could not move her eyes from the ghastly figure on the bed. Glancing over the rest of the body, she saw that both legs were extended at ridiculous angles from the knees, and the arms were similarly askew. Where the man's sexual organs had been, there was only a bloody gash in his groin. The organ lay on the floor near the foot of the bed. She glanced at Yori, who was standing near the far wall.

Yori was calm and looked avidly at the figure that was once a man. His hands were held open in front of him and his mouth was open slightly, so that the fast short breaths that he took caused his relaxed lips to move when he exhaled. His body was lightly splattered with blood; his thumbs were covered with blood to the palms. It left little question in Laura's mind as to how the eyes had gone. Yori also had an erection.

Laura suddenly turned violently away and was sick against the wall. For minutes she heaved, trying to bring up more when there was nothing left to bring up. Staggering out of the room, she fell onto the couch that she had occupied before and began to sob hysterically.

"It's all right now, Doushka," he soothed. "Do not cry now. It is all over."

His voice was like a slap in the face to her. As soon as Laura heard it she was snapped back to reality and began to gain some control over her stomach and breathing. Finally, after a few minutes, she was able to sit with her head thrown back over the top of the couch, in exhausted respite.

"There," Boris said. "You are better now."

"Now you see what I mean when I tell you that it is better to tell us now than later. If you do not tell me the things I must know, I will be forced to bring you back with me, and the others will have no compunction about letting that type of thing happen to you." There was sincerity in his voice. "If you think that that was bad, you should see what Yori can do to a woman," he repeated, although he had not himself ever seen what Yori could do to a woman, but he had heard a great deal about it. He suddenly found himself vowing that someday, he would kill Yori.

"I would tell you, I would, I would." Laura's voice had pleading in it. She knew that whatever they wanted, they would be able to get from her.

"Think! Please think! There must be something that I can go on to get to Pine. You must know something. Where did Bigger find you?"

At the mention of Pine's name, Laura became wide awake and all traces of tremor left her body. She would never tell anything that might lead to his capture by these madmen; the very thought of Pine lying in the same condition as the horror in the other room struck greater fear in her soul than anything that they could do to her.

"There is nothing to . . ." Laura's voice was cut off by a sharp blow across the face.

"I'm not going to play with you any longer," Boris said, shoving her rudely into the back of the couch, and grabbing her shoulder roughly.

As he raised his hand to slap her, Laura struck out valiantly with the fingernails of her right hand, just missing Boris's cheek. The force of her thrust, however, and the instinctive reaction that caused Boris to flinch, freed her shoulder from his grip. Flinging herself from the couch, she raced toward the door, stumbling over displaced furniture and rubble, and came up sharply against the jamb that abutted the door.

Boris leaped from the couch and Yori, who had been standing at the bedroom doorway, dashed over the debris to catch her before she could exit the apartment. Boris reached for her and again she lashed out at him with pointed fingernails. Dodging her hand, Boris grabbed the edge of her other sleeve and pulled her back to him, throwing her forcefully to the ground.

With a sense of futility she looked up at the two men above her and tried to think of something to say, but the germ of last hope was cut off by a sharp movement from Boris.

In the hall, a slight scratching could be heard around the door to Bigger's apartment. Pulling Laura erect by the arm, Boris transported her to the smaller bedroom and tossed her inside. Yori followed and once again that day, Boris shut the door leaving just a crack. With a full view of the entrance to the apartment, Boris watched as the handle on the front door turned slowly and the door opened inward. As the door opened, Boris turned to Laura and smiled.

18

Pine was sure that he would not get far before someone from the hotel caught up with him. The guards were doubtlessly in better shape than he, and could probably run faster. Dashing along the narrow street, he crossed to the opposite side after having passed the truck. Pine then slowed to a fast walk so that he would not seem overly conspicuous to the other pedestrians; he knew that his appearance was bad enough.

Leaving the narrow roadway, Pine passed through several side streets and arrived, after a few minutes, on the Boulevard Saint Germain, near the Metro station at Saint Germain des Près. Slapping his arms about his body to keep warm, he entered the station and gave the female attendant one of the ten little brown second class tickets he had purchased earlier with Laura.

Pine did not feel well. He was cold and raw and had not eaten. He was acutely aware that the police were still looking for him, and it gave him an eerie sensation everytime he saw a distant policeman either coming his way or looking in his direction. He was not cut out to be a fugitive, he reflected, as the train pulled into the station.

The train was relatively crowded for the hour, and not for the first time, Pine wondered what it was that prevented people who purchased second class tickets, from using the red, first class car that loomed so invitingly empty in the center of the train; nobody was there to stop them, and he doubted that the conductors who rarely appeared, checked tickets held by first class riders anyway. He, however, stepped aboard the green second class car. He had decided to take the train to Chatelet and then change to one toward Pont de Neuilly. The stop on that line at Etoile would put him in the vicinity of Bigger's apartment where he hoped to find Laura. He kept thinking about the Deplint woman.

The train finally arrived at Chatelet and Pine alit. Walking toward the Pont de Neuilly train, he saw two policemen who were visually examining the passengers as they moved past. Pine was sure that they were looking for him. After he had nervously walked about ten paces past them, one, who must have noticed his state of disarray, called after him.

Pine did not stop, but took advantage of his lead, and pushing his way past a group of milling children, ran off in the direction of the train he wanted.

The police came after him, and were calling for assistance from the other pedestrians in the tunnel. A large man in laborer's clothing stepped into Pine's path. Pine did not pause for a moment. Gripping his left hand in his right, and pulling in his left shoulder, he hit the man with his shoulder in a football block that sent the Frenchman staggering back against the wall of the tunnel. A second man who had stepped out calling "arrete!" was straight-armed in the chest and knocked on his rear end.

Pine dashed toward the gates that led to the tracks. A train had just pulled in and the automatic gates had already closed, barring further entry to the platform by passengers until the train had departed. Pine knew that if he did not make this train, he would not have the opportunity to catch another. He pushed his way past the five or six people who were waiting patiently for the gates to open. The train had just opened its door and passengers were filing out, those on the platform waiting to enter. A woman was standing guard at the platform gates and a conductor stood by the doors of the train, helping the flow of traffic on and off. Grabbing the top of the gate with both hands, Pine heaved himself up and over in a single motion.

The female guard yelled something, and the conductor turned toward Pine. He could hear the eruption of noise behind him and guessed that the police had arrived. With a last frantic effort, he shoved past the conductor, and threw himself into the train just as the doors began to close.

Fortunately the car was one of the newer models with automatically timed doors; if it had been an older car, the conductor would only have had to reopen the doors to prevent the train from leaving the station. The train started to gain speed just as two puffing policemen pushed their way through the gates onto the platform. Now he worried that the train would be stopped at the next station; he was sure that they had interstation telephones. But there were no police waiting for him when the train arrived at Louvre, and Pine decided to try for the next stop at Palais-Royal. On impulse, however, he pushed through the doors as they started to close. Exiting to the street, he discovered that it had got even colder. Flagging down a cab, Pine directed him to the Étoile. He never did find out if the police were waiting for him at the next station.

Arriving at his destination without further incident he cautiously ascended the stairs. Listening at Bigger's door, he heard some people speaking, but was uncertain whether the voices issued from Bigger's place or the apartment next door. Placing his hand gently on the door knob, he tried to turn it without making any noise, hoping against hope that it would be unlocked. Surprisingly, the knob turned slowly and the door opened. Pine did not remember if Diver had relocked the door when he had left, but he took no chances that a potential enemy would be given warning; swinging the door quickly open, he stepped into an apparently empty apartment. It was in the same condition as when he last had seen it, except that there was a putrid odor.

Entering the main room, disappointed that Laura was not there, he went to check the other rooms. The door to the main bedroom was partially open and he stuck his head inside. Walking uncertainly over to the body, Pine looked down at the face. He had seen death before; he had seen a man killed by a live mortar during field exercises in the Marines. The entire squad had been required to look at the body to teach them what could happen when men were careless. He remembered that the man's head had been partly severed from the body and a limb was missing. Pine had had nightmares for weeks afterward. But this was worse.

This had a cruel direction to its consummation. The bloody holes that had been eye sockets were still oozing blood, so Pine guessed that it had not been long since Bigger had died. Turning away, he let out a short breath. He did not know if it was a breath of relief or of fear. Standing in front of him was Laura. A tall dark man was pointing a gun at her right temple.

"A disturbing sight, is it not, Mr. Pine?" The tall man said with a Russian accent, pointing at the bed with his gun.

"Have they done anything to you, Laura?"

"Do not worry, Mr. Pine," Boris replied. "Nothing as yet

has happened to Miss Kennedy. Her future safety, however, depends upon you." Pine felt his not too solid stomach, after seeing Bigger, sink even lower. "I suggest that we leave the unpleasantness in this room and retire to the living room. There we may continue our discussion." Boris motioned with his weapon.

Righting a few chairs, Boris motioned Pine into the love seat and pushed Laura gently beside him. He pulled one of the chairs over for himself. Yori stood behind another chair and watched.

"Now that I have you both, I am not sure what to do with you," Boris began. "I guess that it would be foolish to kill you outright without attempting to discover what you have been doing of late, wouldn't it?" Boris smiled at them.

"Look," Pine blurted. "Why don't you let the girl go? She doesn't know anything."

Boris laughed. "You Americans are so romantic. Do you think that this is the proper thing to say, or do you say it because you think that we are such fools?"

Pine silently cursed Diver and then began on King. He cursed himself. He cursed everything that had led to his meeting Laura. If he had never met her, she would never have got into this mess and now she was going to suffer because of him.

"Listen," Pine tried again. "I'm only a lawyer who was asked to do something for the Embassy here in Paris. I don't know anything. They wouldn't tell me anything. In fact, I had to escape myself, in order to get up here."

Boris did not pay any attention to Pine's remonstrations. He had walked over to the window and pondered the situation. He looked at his watch and turning to Yori, said something in Russian.

Pulling Pine to his feet and hauling Laura after him, Boris led the two to the door and started them towards the elevator.

Laura scrambled into her coat, as much to cover her soiled clothing as for warmth. Pine assumed that they were being taken somewhere safer for interrogation, and he knew that if they were to make an escape, it would have to be either now or during the trip to wherever they were going. He hoped that it would not be necessary to get into a physical conflict with the man in black; it would be no contest.

Neither the elevator ride nor the short walk to the car had provided an opportunity for escape. Boris guided them into the back seat, and Yori got into the front with him. Yori, holding the pistol pointed directly at Laura's kneecap, kept his eyes carefully on Pine. Boris turned to the couple in the back of the car.

"Please do nothing foolish. Yori will not kill you, but you will be painfully disabled. It is better to remain healthy, yes?" He ordered them to turn around and sit on the floor with their feet on the seats. He then tied their hands behind them and put blinders over their eyes. Again he warned them about foolishness and the car lurched forward. Pine wondered if foolishness included wetting his pants; he was almost that scared.

19

Leaving the Hotel de Chance, Diver and King drove back to the Right Bank. They intended to stop at the Embassy to check in with French, and then to return to the Hotel Bristol. Diver hoped that Bigger's people would act quickly so that this matter could be closed out. It was presumed that the Soviets did not know that Central Intelligence had intervened, and would assume that the search of Bigger's apartment had been made by Pine when they located his wallet in the living room where it had been left. Although it might seem an obvious plant, other information that had been dropped in the city would support it, and, of course, Pine would be at the hotel. Diver was sure that the police would not have access to the sources that would provide the tips, but Bigger would.

French, who was just leaving the building, met them in the courtyard. "I'm starved. How about joining me for lunch?"

"Good idea," King replied. "We can go somewhere quiet and get a few things settled."

The three men walked through the court in front of the Embassy and into the street, turning left towards Place de la Concorde. They turned into one of the narrow side streets and entered a café. It was late for lunch and only a few diners remained when they entered. They took a table near the rear of the café and placed their orders.

"How's Pine taking his solitude?" French asked around a mouthful of the bread that had been placed on the table when they were seated.

"As well as can be expected, I suppose," countered Diver. "He's a pretty active guy, you know, and didn't like the idea of being shelved."

"You can't blame him really," King remarked. "He probably feels less nervous when he's active. Keeps his mind off the danger."

"It seems that the only chance we have of getting to Bigger quickly is to lay a trail straight to Pine. If Bigger thinks that Pine is set to blow his cover, he's sure to come after him. The only problem is to set it up so that the police won't get there first."

"You'd better be careful how you cast the scent," French commented. "Bigger's been on my staff for a few years now, and the one thing I've learned about him is that he's clever."

"We figure that he can't take too many precautions now. He's got to act quickly if he hopes to get to Pine before anyone else does. And he's got to move before the Ruskies come down on him as well. Does he know that you're back yet, French?" King looked over at the Security Officer.

"I don't think so. Why?"

"Well, if he does get word that you're back," King answered, "it'll give him another incentive to apply the jets. If the cops get to Pine first, they'll notify the Embassy and with you

153

back, he'll lose his chance to get Pine before he's interrogated, since you'd be the one to be present, not him. That'll mean he'll have to get to Pine before the cops."

"Maybe we can let it slip that French has returned?" Diver suggested. "That shouldn't be too difficult."

"It's probably unnecessary; by the time Bigger heard, he already should have found Pine," French said. "Besides, he doesn't need any further motivation, you can be sure. What's your next step?"

"I think we'll head back to the Bristol to see if the Kennedy girl is happy and smiling," Diver replied. "Then we'll orchestrate the details from there."

After the men had eaten, they went their separate ways. When they arrived at the hotel, Diver and King went directly to their rooms. Laura failed to answer their knock, and Diver, using his key, unlocked the door and stepped in ahead of King. In the center of the sitting room, the food sat uneaten on the tray. Diver exchanged glances with King and then made a dash towards the bedroom calling Laura's name. King went in the other direction towards the door adjoining his room. Picking up the house phone and dialing the desk, King glanced over the untouched lunch.

"Why would she order lunch and then not eat it? And she was instructed not to leave the room."

"I hope nothing has happened here. Pine will never forgive us for this one." Diver answered distractedly.

The desk clerk answered the phone and in response to King's questions, replied that, yes, Ma'amselle Kennedy did order lunch and no, he did not know who had brought it up, but he could find out for them. He expressed hope that nothing was wrong. King asked if he had seen the girl leave the hotel. The clerk explained that she had left, a while ago, with Monsieur Harrison, whom, he added, he was sure Monsieur Diver would remember from school, since they were old school friends. Repeating the statement to Diver, King side-stepped as Diver made a rush for the instrument.

"What did this Harrison look like?" Diver asked into the phone.

"Why, he was very fat, and rather well-dressed, Monsieur. But it is strange, because a short time ago, the same questions were asked by your other friend who came in with you this morning."

Diver thanked the clerk and hung up the phone.

"We've bought it now," Diver remarked to King. "Bigger's got her. Do you think he would bring her back to his flat?"

"There's only one way to find out."

Taking the stairs instead of the elevator, they rushed into the street in front of the hotel. Grabbing the first cab that they could find and giving the driver Bigger's address, they sat back looking worried. Neither wanted any harm to come to the girl; neither wanted to be the one to tell Pine.

The cab pulled up in front of the apartment, and Diver, paying the driver, suggested that they be careful not to give Bigger any warning, if he was there, that they were coming. Taking the stairs again, they moved silently to the apartment.

Knocking at the door, the two men waited tensely for a response. After a reasonable interval, they knocked again. Diver looked at King. He shrugged, and again removed his burglar tools from the jacket pocket. Opening the door, the two men stepped into the mess that they had created a few short hours before. There did not seem to be any change in the room, although King felt sure that he had overturned the small love seat that was set upright at the far end of the room. Looking around, they saw Pine's wallet still lying where they had left it. Then King saw the remains of someone's dinner staining the carpeting behind the love seat. With a dash, the two men raced to inspect the other rooms. Diver found it.

Staring quietly, Diver called King into the bedroom.

155

"My God!" Diver said, appalled. "What a mess. Only a madman could have done that to him."

Looking unaffectedly at the ruined figure, King shook his head.

"They must really have had it in for him to do a thing like this. I'd hate to meet the guy who did it, though."

"I wouldn't," Diver commented with venom.

"I wonder where the hell the girl is?" King said, looking perplexed.

"We'd better check this place out thoroughly before we leave. They might have left a clue to where they were going."

Turning the already dishevelled apartment inside out added nothing to their knowledge. Fearful of using the phone on the chance that the Russians may have tapped it, they left the apartment and reported to French on the first phone they could find.

French took a moment to get to the telephone, and when he did, he sounded agitated. Diver agitated him further; he told him about Bigger and the missing girl. Then French dropped his bomb; he told Diver about Pine. There was a painful silence at each end of the line. Finally Diver turned to King and told what he had just learned.

"How the hell did he slip away from those guards of yours?" Diver asked into the phone, rather testily. "There's no place he could go."

"Apparently he slipped out through a bathroom window. The guard had a hard enough time telling me."

"I'll just bet he did," Diver answered. "Well, what do we do now?"

French was silent for a moment.

"We can cry a lot," he suggested.

It was agreed that the three of them would meet at the Hotel de Chance immediately to see if they could pick up some of the pieces. Finding a cab, Diver and King rushed to the small Left Bank hotel to find French impatiently waiting. He had finished questioning the guard who was on duty and had got no more from him than on the telephone.

"You can't really blame the guy," French remarked, referring to the guard. "What the hell was he supposed to do? Hold Pine's hand in the can?

"You've got to hand it to that bastard," French added. "He's a slippery sonofabitch. He must have found out about the Kennedy girl's disappearance when he called the Bristol. Then he went out the toilet window and onto the roof next door. The guards out back said that they had their eyes on the court. There were five of them so I doubt that all five could have missed him if he went the back way. He must have come down the front when he was shielded by traffic, because the trellis had been pulled down, which would tend to support that theory."

"Well, where could he have gone after that?" King was reflective. "He didn't know anyplace in Paris that Bigger might return to with the girl except for Bigger's apartment."

They stopped speaking abruptly, the three of them speculating simultaneously. The idea that Pine had worked Bigger over passed through each mind at the same instant.

"Of course he wouldn't do a thing like that. He couldn't. Besides, he probably didn't have the time." King answered to their silent question.

"I don't think that he could have done it either," Diver remarked. "You didn't see it, French. It was incredible."

"Besides," King proposed. "The timing's all wrong. That man had been dead for at least an hour before we arrived. If it had been Pine who killed him, the body would still have been warm. And, after all, he's got to be able to come back to us; we're the only ones who can clear him with the police."

Discarding the idea that Pine had killed Bigger, they again began to consider where he could have gone. It was suggested that if Pine had found Bigger dead, he might also have found a clue to where the girl had been taken. Perhaps, he had even found her there and taken her with him. If so, they hoped that he would have the sense to call the Embassy and leave a message for Diver or King.

As the three were speculating, a car stopped in front of the hotel and two men got out. They walked purposefully towards the entrance, stepped through the door, and stopped. Diver looked at them with wide eyes. One ot the men returned his gaze.

"Oh no!" Diver gasped.

20

The Director of the *Deuxième Bureau* sat behind his desk in the small office allotted to him. His job was particularly thankless these days. Because of de Gaulle's new policy of self-determination, the extent of security had increased, but the sources of information had dried up; no longer were the files of Great Britain and the United States fully open to him. And the Soviet Union, with whom France was supposed to have become closer, still maintained strict security over her files.

Sitting back, the Chief removed his rimless glasses and rubbed his eyes with the fingertips of both hands. The papers that cluttered his desk swam in confusion before his tired eyes. The newest mess was that created by the American, Pine, and his sudden disappearance. Where could he have disappeared to? Neither the police nor his own operatives had found any trace that led to him, and the chase had been on for almost twenty-four hours. He wished that the Department of Defense had given him a more detailed briefing on this matter, but they had repeated, as usual for the military, "need to know, need to know." He thought that only Security could pull that line; times had changed in France.

The buzzer on his desk jerked him out of his reveries. His secretary told him that Inspector Devereau was on the phone. After he replaced the receiver he asked his secretary to have Pomey and Cambert in his office within the hour. When the two agents arrived, the Director could see that they too had not slept much recently. Inspector Devereau was sitting on one side of the little room smoking a tiny cigarette stub, and he was introduced to the two men.

"The Inspector has some information that may be of interest to us," the Director said. "It appears that a woman heard some strange activities in the apartment next to hers this morning, and called the police. When they investigated, they found that it was rented by an American named Charles Bigger. He was with the American Embassy here in Paris. Now he is dead."

Neither Pomey nor Cambert showed any expression when they received the news. They were in possession of sufficient information regarding activities at the American Embassy to know who Bigger was, but they reserved comment until the Director had finished.

"I might mention that the manner in which he died indicates that it was neither accidental nor simple murder. The apartment had also been searched by experts."

"After we saw it," Devereau commented, "we decided that it would be better if you fellows handled this case because of possible security implications. We have not yet contacted the Americans."

"Quite right," the Director said.

"Have you searched the apartment?" Pomey asked.

"No," Devereau replied. "We made a routine inspection, but nothing in detail. Besides, since we suspected it was a political hit, we did not want to disturb anything until you people could see the rooms. We're not sure what it may be that you are looking for."

"Well, let's get up there now," Cambert suggested. "You'll come with us, I hope, Inspector?"

"Indeed," Devereau answered.

The Director made a note on a desk pad and indicated that the interview was over.

"Let me know immediately, if you discover anything," he interjected. "No matter where I am, have the call put through. If nothing turns up, come back here directly. We'll notify the Americans ourselves, Inspector, after our search."

"Very good, Sir," the Inspector replied deferentially.

The Inspector picked up his hat and turned towards the door. He was followed by Pomey and Cambert, who glanced back at the Director knowingly. In front of the building, a police car waited, and the three men sped towards the apartment where Bigger's body lay. A police officer was standing at the entrance to the building. He nodded to Devereau as he entered the house with the two Security men. They took the elevator to the third floor and were greeted by another police officer at the door to the apartment. The officer opened the door without a word.

The furniture, still scattered about the rooms, had been untouched by the police, and Pomey was surprised both by its richness and by the contrasting disarray.

"They must pay these Americans well. This is not the apartment of a public servant," Devereau said.

"Yes," Cambert replied, thinking, unless the public servant was serving more than one public.

Walking to the bedroom with Devereau, Pomey con-

161

sidered that this might have been the defector at the Embassy, upon whom the wrath of either one of his employers had been visited. Pomey thought that it was probably not the Americans, as they usually did not work this way. After he had seen the body he was not sure who could have done it; the Russians did not work this way either, in his experience. Cambert grabbed a sheet out of a drawer from which it hung, and draped it over the body.

"It looks like he's been dead for several hours," Pomey stated. "This looks like a professional job. Perverted, but professional. I doubt that we'll find anything here to implicate anyone."

Returning to the living room, the men began a casual look at the shattered remains of the apartment. The police had already sent for a photographer and a fingerprint expert.

Suddenly, Cambert called the other men over to the foot of the couch. Hidden at the foot of the settee was a wallet. Picking it up carefully with his handkerchief, Pomey flipped it open.

"Looks like we might have something to go on at that," he remarked, looking at the name on an hotel receipt that was stuck in an inner fold.

The three looked at each other and Cambert smiled broadly at Devereau.

"Isn't this the man you've been hunting?" Devereau queried.

"Yes," Pomey responded. "This is our first lead. I think we'll check out this hotel, and see what we can find."

The Minister of Defense and the First Secretary sat in a comfortably furnished room. They were speaking with the Director of the *Deuxième Bureau*. After the Director had received his report from Pomey, he had contacted the others and was instructed to appear for an audience.

"I would not have bothered you at this time," the Minister said, "but we find ourselves in an awkward position."

A secretary entered, carrying a tray containing a bottle of wine and three glasses. All conversation stopped as he poured the rich red liquid into the glasses and passed them around. The Director took a sip and cleared his throat.

"When I advised you that the American might have had this intelligence, you told me to keep you informed of our progress at all stages of the investigation," the Director said. "You said that the document was of vital importance to us, which I will not question, although you never told me why. I am aware that it contains information about Russian missile sites, but I do not understand how this could be of such importance to us, that it would justify the risks we must take to secure it."

The Secretary looked over to the Minister for a moment, and then back to the Director.

"We expected that it would come to this, Paul," he said. "It was our hope that you would find what we needed; then no explanation would have been necessary. But it now appears that we will have to tell you something about our present military objectives. You understand that this is all on a strictly high level security basis involving Defense, or you would have been briefed before.

"You are aware, of course, that one of the reasons we have entered into relations with Moscow has been to balance the power structure in Europe and the world, with France more effectively situated at its center. You also realize that it was our hope to acquire some military technology from Moscow. This plan has not worked out as well as we had thought.

"As a result, we have gained nothing from our Soviet allies, except the animosity of our European neighbors, not to mention the United States. Our prime aim was to obtain the missile technology that we sorely lack, with which to enter the international arena and, perhaps, establish ourselves as a major Western power in Europe; then we could dilute American influence over NATO. You do realize that we have, at present, no long-range missiles of our own. But Russia has not cooperated at all.

"At the same time, our interests in other parts of the globe have induced us to enter into other concords. These have not been so well-publicized, thank God, and are, in fact, only known to a few of our top government officials. Since it involved Defense, and was out of your sphere of operations, your Department was never privy.

"One of our largest sources of rubber has traditionally been Vietnam, particularly the North, where we have numerous large plantations, owned by French nationals. After Geneva and SEATO, we were obliged to dispose of these holdings when the Vietnamese nationals were in a position to buy us out.

"In an attempt to protect our holdings, we entered into an agreement with the North Vietnamese to supply advisors and provide military training; in return, we retain our holdings, although not in our names. We felt that the Americans could never win, based upon our own experiences in that sphere. Besides, we knew that Russian interests would work to deter an American victory, and that in time, the American people would tire of the war, and will someday create enough trouble to add another element of confusion to the problems of South East Asia, and help cover our activities.

"Now, here's the problem we face." The Minister lit a cigarette. "The Americans do not know the extent of our involvement there. If they knew, it could become embarrassing for us throughout the world. It is naturally in our own interests that we prevent their discovering our . . . shall we say, relationships. In addition, we have not yet obtained what we require in long-range missile technology. If, however, we had access to the Soviet missiles, we could study them and, perhaps, learn enough to develop our own. Our only source of such a weapon is Vietnam; we have the military personnel there and Russia has the missiles. But we do not know the location of the sites. This is the crux. The American is said to have such a list; we must get it."

The Director sat back and pondered what he had just learned. He was not too sure that he liked the idea of antagonizing Washington. During the Second World War it was the Americans who had done so much so willingly to help the Republic. He also knew that the Soviets were too self-interested and could not be relied upon for a long-term alliance. The Director felt, as did many Frenchmen, that the future of his country lay not in military acquisitions, but in an economic alliance that would lead to a solidarity indefatigable in the face of any Eastern nation.

"Well, if we find Pine, we will get whatever information he may have," he said. "You don't have to worry about that."

"That's not what we're worried about," the Secretary interposed. "After his interrogation, he can not be allowed to expose our knowledge or intent; even his suspicions would be destructive to our interests. We can not chance that Washington will question why we are so interested in this matter. You can be sure that with a little push in the right direction, and some concentrated effort, they will flush our operation.

"When you are finished with Mr. Pine," the Secretary said softly, "he must be terminated."

"Don't you think that's going a bit far?" the Director asked incredulously. "And what if we take him and he has no information?"

The two men gazed at the Director for a moment and then lowered their eyes. The Director knew that the interview was over. He had got his orders.

After reporting to the Director's office, Pomey returned

with the Inspector to bring in for questioning the woman who had phoned the Prefecture. He was told that an "interdepartmental" snag would be blamed for any delay in advising the American authorities of Bigger's death, and that he should proceed with his investigation as quickly as possible. The last words from the Director had been that whatever happened, Pomey was to keep the Americans out of it.

Considering their next step, Pomey and Cambert decided that a quick look at the hotel in the Left Bank would be appropriate. The receipt that they had found in Pine's wallet was dated that day, and it was likely that he was still there.

They obtained a Bureau car and drove over. They had a feeling that this might be the step that concluded their part in the operation; they both needed sleep, and would not get any until Pine was in custody. Leaving the car parked on the sidewalk so traffic could pass, they entered the building. It took only a few seconds for Pomey to realize that the entire operation had fallen to pieces.

21

One of the things that made Diver's job interesting was that he met and knew many operatives from other countries; the alleged secretiveness of all intelligence operations was not the rule. It was relatively easy for a country to use a man once or twice on a foreign mission, but after that, he became known. This in itself did not impair his effectiveness as an agent, because his value was measured in the quality of his work. Agents were taught to be investigators, and the areas in which they delved were merely outside the scope of normal police jurisdiction; the subject matter was not necessarily criminal, but involved information-gathering. Naturally, there were jobs that required a higher degree of secrecy, and for those, agents were brought in from other arenas, or a special operative was used whose identity was judiciously guarded. These were the people who filled the more popular conception of the "spy." For missions that required no special skills, but needed anonymity, civilians who had sufficient clearance were sometimes used because their cover was ideal. Mark Pine had been selected for just that reason.

During the years that Diver had served with the government, he had encountered many operatives employed by European nations; he could usually tell how seriously interested a country was in a program by the agent assigned.

When he saw the two men entering the Hotel de Chance, Diver knew immediately that the Republic of France had a deeply vested interest in this operation.

"Jacques!" Diver said calmly. "And what brings you here this fine afternoon?"

Pomey was equally surprised to see Diver, but for different reasons.

"Hello, Percy."

"Well, I repeat," Diver said. "What the hell are *you* doing *here?*"

"It's still my country, you know," Pomey interposed with a smile. "I might ask you the same."

French, who had been standing in the background with King, and who knew Pomey as well, stepped forward.

"It seems like old home week," Pomey said. "And how are you, Monsieur French?"

The three men faced each other, not knowing quite what to say next.

"You know, of course, about our fugitive American, Pomey?" French asked.

"Yes. We have been looking for him ourselves."

"We have too, as you can imagine." Diver took the lead, following French's direction. "It's quite embarrassing to us that an American has been involved in a double killing here in Paris, especially considering the deterioration of the relations between our respective nations."

"Ah, yes." Pomey looked thoughtful for a moment. "But why have they sent you, Diver? Are you not too important for so simple a matter as murder?"

"Well, actually, the victims were not that innocent, as I'm sure you know. Those two Germans, I mean."

"How did you know that?"

"You're not the only country with agents, you know," Diver added. "Now, as I said, how come a big shot like you got this particular assignment?"

"We have never said that your American was the killer. We are only interested in questioning him. That's all. As to what I am doing here, I am searching for this Pine. My trail, it led here."

Diver knew that he had set a trap to catch Bigger and that it had backfired. Bigger was dead, but Pomey, who could not have known that the trail was a plant, must have got on to it after finding Bigger's body and the wallet that had been left in the apartment. The trail did lead to the Hotel de Chance. That there was no other trail was strong evidence that Pomey knew about Bigger. It was even likely that he believed Pine to be the killer.

It also bothered Diver that the Bureau had put Pomey into the game. There was no reason for him to be involved in such an investigation unless the matter was more important to the French than Washington had believed. The French should not have been interested in Soviet missile sites located in Nam. And yet they had assigned one of their top operatives to the case.

Being seen disturbed Diver as well. The French were now sure to know that the job involved more serious matters than murder. Whatever the French suspected, they knew now.

"We'd better get inside, Jacques," Diver said, leading Pomey and his associate into the lobby of the small hotel. Calling the concierge, Diver asked her if he could speak with the others privately. She led them to a small vacant room on the ground floor.

Diver walked over to the casement window that was dark gray with dust and soot. Making small circles on the grimy pane with his finger, he waited until the others had seated themselves on the iron fourposter. King stood against the wall near the door.

"We have worked together before, Jacques, and I will not lie to you," he lied. Diver had decided to tell Pomey as much of the truth as he could; at least as much of the truth as the French already knew. "The fact is, we suspect that one of our people at the Embassy has defected. Despite your back-scratching with Moscow, I don't think you'd like them to have what's been passing over. Pine appears to have been working with the defector, and it was during one of the pickups that the two Germans were killed. I'm here to see if we can locate the defector, who, incidentally, seems to have disappeared as well. I can't tell you more, but that's it in a nutshell."

Diver figured that Pomey knew about Bigger's death, and he probably knew that Bigger was connected with the Embassy by now. By telling what he did, Pomey would be able to deduce only what already was suspected; that Bigger was a defector, and that Pine was his killer. Now, if Pomey were on the level himself, he would tell Diver that Bigger had been killed, since he would assume Diver knew nothing about it. By what he was *not* told, Diver would know more accurately how deeply French interests were vested.

Pomey heard Diver's story and decided that it explained the surface facts. He knew that there had been a defector at the American Embassy, although he had not been sure who. Lying dead in his apartment, Bigger was the likely candidate. But Pine and Bigger working together did not ring true. It must have been the defector who had had Pine's room searched at the Candide, and if Bigger was both the defector and Pine's contact, he would not have had to do that. Pomey decided the story would have to do until he could think about it.

"What was the nature of the intelligence that Pine was to deliver?" Pomey asked.

"You know damn well that I can't tell you that, but it's one of the reasons I'm here. We're not really sure. We were in the process of coming down on Bigger when the shit hit the fan."

Again, Pomey wondered how much to believe. He would have to assume that it was untrue until he could check up and see what else Diver had done since his arrival in Paris.

"Pine is not here, I presume?" Pomey changed the subject.

"We just got here a few minutes before you. He was gone."

"What made you come to the hotel in the first place?" Pomey inquired.

"We got a call from one of our streetmen who fell on a lead," Diver said, knowing that there was sufficient evidence on the street to pinpoint Pine; he had planted it. Diver paused for a moment. "By the time we got here, Pine had already slipped away."

There was silence in the room for a full minute.

"How did *you* find out about Pine being here?" Diver finally said, watching Pomey's face carefully.

"Oh, well, we checked through police registration. His name had been filed earlier by the concierge."

"I see." Diver saw. They must have seen the wallet at Bigger's apartment after he and King had left.

"Well," Pomey said, after a pause. "We'd better be getting back to our office. If we could just see Pine's room first," he added as they went to the door.

"Yes, of course." Diver called the concierge and Pomey explained what he wanted in fast and fluid French. As Pomey started up the stairs, the elderly lady held up her hand and rubbed her thumb against the first two fingers a few times. Diver got the message.

On the way up the stairs, Pomey questioned the woman about Pine.

"Oui, Monsieur," she replied in French. "He arrived this morning and told me that he did not have the time to fill out the cards, but will do it when he returns. He gives me a few days' rent in advance, so what do I care. Listen, my friend, I do not violate the law. If I get my cards to the Prefecture by the evening, what do I care when they are filled out, yes?"

Pomey almost choked on the story. He realized that she probably told the same tale to Diver, so he would know that the cards, which Pomey supposedly relied upon to find Pine, had not yet been filed with the police. That Diver had seen him here was bad enough, but now that he also knew that Pomey had lied to him, Diver's already aroused suspicions would become inflamed.

"Does the American gentleman know that the cards have not yet been deposited with the police?" Pomey knew the answer, but he had to ask.

The woman looked slyly at the Frenchman. She knew that if she lied and was found out, she would be in serious trouble.

"Oui, Monsieur. They also asked the same question."

After seeing the empty room, Pomey began to suspect that the trail had been a plant; nobody had lived there for a while, judging by the dust. He could not understand why it had been done, but he was sure that Pine was not registered at that hotel, and that he was working for Washington, probably to help retrieve the list from the defector. Then, perhaps, Bigger had not been killed by Pine. If that were the case, who had killed him?

Diver returned to the American Embassy with King and French.

"What now?" French asked.

"I think we'd better punt," Diver submitted. "I haven't got

the foggiest where Pine could have got to. We may have to wait until he calls us. I think we'd better put someone on the French. They know a hell of a lot more than they're telling. We may be able to get a line if we bug them and see what comes in respecting either Pine or Bigger."

"You're probably right." King was sitting back, playing with an ashtray made out of an old mortar casing. "When I get hold of our 007 friend, I'm going to kick his ass for him."

"I just hope that he has one to kick when we do find him," Diver interjected.

Pomey and Cambert entered the Director's office uncertainly. He was busily at work on some papers when they were shown in.

"Well, how did it go?" he asked without looking up.

"Not as well as one might hope," Cambert said.

The Chief looked up. Peering sharply at Pomey and then at Cambert, he began to feather the corner of a filing card with his fingernail.

"What does that mean?"

"We went to the hotel. Pine was not there; in fact, I don't think he was ever there. We met some American Intelligence people at the hotel. You remember Percy Diver and that fellow French from the Embassy?"

"You'd better tell me exactly what happened, from the beginning."

Pomey started from the time he first saw Diver standing in the small hotel, and gave the substance of their conversations.

"What do you plan to do next?"

"I was hoping that you had a suggestion," Pomey admitted.

"Well, I hate to do it, but I think we are going to have to wait for the Americans to make a move. We'll have to put a bug or something on their lines and wait until something comes in. Then we'll have to get there first."

"You figure that they actually know where Pine is, and are hiding him?"

"It's possible. If they don't, he'll be coming to them soon enough. Where else can he go? As soon as he contacts them, we move in."

The Director scraped his chair back and looked at Pomey for a while. Finally he frowned and began to rub his eyes.

"Look, Pomey. I know that you have worked with Diver in the past. When this thing breaks, it might be necessary for you to clean up the loose ends. That includes Pine, this fellow King, French, and Diver. Do you think you'll be able to do it?"

"I can do it."

22

Pine sat on the floor of the car, facing the rear of the vehicle, his feet propped up on the back seat. Laura sat beside him in the same position. Every time the car hit a bump or a chuckhole, the back of his head slammed into the metal trim that ran across the seat behind him.

They drove for about an hour, during which time Pine's anger faded and his fears grew. Alone, he was sure that he could fend for himself. If it came to that, he would die, but not without a fight. With Laura around, however, he had to be more careful; he did not want her to be harmed.

The car finally rolled to a halt. Boris got out while Yori remained in place, the gun leveled at Laura's stomach. Boris opened the door and roughly pulled her from the back seat. Pine called her name.

"Don't worry about your little friend," Boris answered.

"She will be cared for as long as you don't try anything heroic."

Yori climbed out of the car, and grabbing Laura by the arm, guided her towards the house in front of which they had stopped. Pine was herded after them by Boris.

They walked into the chateau and across the hall to the large room in which Shaskof waited. On Shaskof's command, he ushered the prisoners into the room. Placing Yori's gun on a small table, he turned to the small man behind the desk.

"Bigger has been taken care of," he said. "Miss Kennedy," he said, indicating the girl, "was there with him and Pine came afterwards, looking for her. I thought there might be something you could get from them."

Boris's hands were clammy. He was never sure what to expect from Shaskof. All he kept remembering was that he had been ordered not to return until the job had been finished.

"Have they told you anything?" Shaskof asked.

"Nothing yet," Boris replied.

"Remove the blindfolds and untie them, Yori," Shaskof instructed. "I want to see their faces."

Pine spent a few moments blinking in the sudden glare of light. Through tear-glazed lids, he surveyed the room. Laura was also adjusting to the light and had calmly begun to remove her coat. As he inspected the room, his eyes fell upon the man behind the desk.

"My name is Shaskof, Mr. Pine. I have a job to do. If you force me to be brutal, I shall be brutal. But it is not necessary. You will speak in the end anyway, and why subject yourself to these vulgarities? I would suggest that we sit down with a drink and some dinner and get this over with. What do you say?"

The idea of food reminded Pine of how long it had been since he had eaten. He was almost tempted.

"Screw you," he answered sullenly.

Pine waited for a blow. None came. Instead, Shaskof exhaled a long sigh and nodded to Boris. Pine and Laura were taken by the arm and conducted to a side door which opened upon a flight of stone steps leading to the cellar. Yori preceded them down the stairs. They walked along a corridor to another door which was chained and padlocked. Fishing a key from his pocket, Yori opened the lock and rattled the chain from the clamps through which it was strung. They passed through the door and the corridor in which they now found themselves, led through a wine cellar, the racks of which were partially filled with bottles coated with dust and cobwebs. A large rat scampered across the floor.

The corridor ended at another passageway that led down what appeared to be a ramp to a lower level. At the bottom of the ramp, they turned right and were guided to the far end of a hallway where a door loomed invitingly open. They were shoved into the room and the door was slammed behind them with a metallic clang. Pine heard a scraping as a lock was made fast and then footsteps receding.

The room was about fifteen feet by twenty. The walls and ceiling were constructed of gray stone and there were no windows. The door through which they had come was made of rusted and pitted iron. Near the ceiling, a small vent was built into the wall. It was about six inches square, and a greenish slime hung from its grilled mouth. From somewhere, a hollow, resounding drip echoed through the chamber. Overhead, a single, bare bulb hung from a wire, casting a dim light and accenting each corner with shadows. There was no light switch in the room and Pine supposed that it worked from outside. The room was devoid of furniture, and the floor was made of the same rough stone as the walls and ceiling. The cell was damp, cold, and unappealing, with a musty smell that reminded Pine of the rat he had seen in the corridor. Walking to the entranceway, Pine grabbed the rusty handle and placed his good shoulder against the pitted surface. The solid metal did not even creak under his full weight.

Laura was standing directly under the harsh lamp in the center of the cell. Her arms were wrapped around her body and she was shivering. Pine came over to her and put his arms about her tenderly.

"Don't be frightened, sweetheart," he said. "We'll get out of this somehow."

"Did you see what that monster did to Mr. Bigger?" she said. "What if he tries to do that to us?"

"We'll worry about that when the time comes. Why don't you tell me what happened since we left you this morning," he suggested.

Laura began, and by the time she had reached the part where Bigger brought her to his apartment, she was sobbing. Pine kept his arm tightly around her shoulders trying to soothe her. He had placed his jacket beneath them on the hard stone floor, and they were sitting close together.

When she had finished, Pine sat for a while in thought. Before he had left the Hotel de Chance, he had called the Bristol and spoken with the clerk. Although he had left no message, he was sure that Diver would learn about the call when he discovered that Laura was missing and that he had escaped. He was sure to start a search for them; but what could Pine expect them to find? They would not know for sure that he had gone to Bigger's apartment. And even if they did figure that out, all they would find would be Bigger's body and no clue to where they had been taken. They would not even be sure who had taken them. Pine accepted that they were on their own, but what they could do about it was beyond him. Before Pine could fully collect his thoughts, the door rattled and swung inward. Shaskof was standing at the entrance with Yori at his back. Boris was in the background, looking dejected.

"We are through wasting time, Mr. Pine," Shaskof remarked. "Although Boris is not enthusiastic, Yori is looking forward to experimenting with you."

"What do you want from us?" Pine asked with resignation. "I don't know anything. I was just a courier, that's all."

"Oh come, now, Mr. Pine," Shaskof gushed. "You are too modest. Why don't you tell us exactly what you remember from the list that was taken from you? We would also like to know whom you have told and the names of all your contacts in Paris. As we have you here now we might as well make use of you. Perhaps, we will even learn something that we do not already know."

"What the hell do you think I am, a walking directory for the C.I.A.?" Shaskof grinned back at him.

"But I didn't remember anything from the list. I looked at it once. I remember only that it dealt with missile sites in Vietnam, but I couldn't remember those long Oriental names if I tried. I swear it."

"Mr. Pine, Mr. Pine," Shaskof chortled. "You really surprise me. You really do. How can you expect me to believe such a story when my agents have seen you travelling about Paris with Diver, who is known to be an American agent. When Bigger told us that he had selected you from civilian files, and that he would have no trouble with you, we were suspicious. We knew that Washington was getting close to him, and we suspected that he had been duped, and that you had been selected to compromise him. The events, as they occurred, have justified our suspicions. Mr. Pine, you are a professional American agent, from which theater of operations, I do not know, but there must be a great deal about your organization that you can tell us."

Leading them to another room down a different passageway, Shaskof spoke in lowered tones to Yori, who murmured back monosyllabic grunts. The new chamber was identical to

179

the first, but contained four chairs and a long surgical table.

Yori pushed both Pine and the girl into two of the chairs, and stepped back to speak with Shaskof again. Then he approached Pine and hit him hard across the face. Laura cried out. Pine said nothing. Yori's large hand came back across Pine's face again and a small rivulet of blood crept from the corner of his mouth. Laura had closed her eyes.

Pulling Pine rudely from the chair, Yori shoved him against the wall and tied his hands over his head to a metal loop that hung from the wall on a swivel. With a regular rhythm, Yori pounded Pine's stomach and rib cage with his huge fists. At first, Pine tried to keep his stomach muscles tight, but after the first few blows, a fist caught him in the *solar plexus,* and his wind rushed out with a gasp; so did his resolve. With his head bobbing and mouth agape to catch such air as he could, he felt his bruised ribs grow from pain to pain. He was sure that they were being shattered. Finally unconscious, he slumped forward.

Yori ripped Pine's shirt off and turned him to face the wall. Taking a ceramic bowl of cold water, he sloshed it across Pine's back. Pine's head swung up as awareness slowly returned. Yori took out a long cigar. Laura's eyes followed him as he lit it and slowly drew on it, until the tip was a deep, angry red glow.

Pine could see nothing. His vision was blurred by pain and his consciousness was uncertain. Every time he coughed, he tasted blood. As awareness returned, his first sensation was not of pain, but of severe cold. His body was wet and he had begun to shiver uncontrollably. Then he heard Yori in the background lighting what sounded like a match. He swung his head around as far as it would turn, but with his hands tied above his head, his shoulders blocked his view. Suddenly he felt a sharp stinging sensation on his back where his arm met his shoulder. The stinging billowed into a gigantic shock wave of agony, as his entire back seemed to snap aflame with a violent hissing of flesh and water. He screamed. The pressure on his back relaxed, but the pain continued. Then he felt it on the other side. The pain leaped up to his neck and down to his groin, radiating from the tiny spot where hell was let loose. After the cigar was removed from his skin, red embers continued to cling to his flesh, slowly fading as perspiration extinguished them. Yori was about to place the lit end of the cigar for a third time, when Shaskof stopped him.

"Wait a moment, Yori." Shaskof walked over to Pine, and twisted his face around by the hair so he could look at his face. Shaskof swept some of the perspiration from Pine's forehead, and wiped it off on one of the burn marks. Pine bellowed as the salty liquid was pressed into his burns.

"Mr. Pine," Shaskof started. "Please won't you tell us something now?"

Pine's pleading eyes spoke volumes; his mouth said nothing. Choking on what tasted like blood, he tried to repeat that he knew nothing. He could not make his voice work.

Turning to Yori, Shaskof nodded towards the girl.

"Try your talents on her, Yori. Let Mr. Pine watch for a while. Perhaps that will loosen his constipated tongue."

Shaskof left the room as Yori cut Pine down from the wall and threw him into one of the chairs. Boris left with a gray look on his face, as Shaskof returned holding a glass of the most beautiful clear liquid Pine had ever seen; his tongue touched his parched lips in anticipation. Looking at Pine before he took a sip, Shaskof frowned.

"You're not thirsty, are you, Mr. Pine?" He looked at the glass and poured a bit of its contents onto the floor. Laughing, he said, "Well, we are not so uncivilized. Here, have your drink."

Pine grabbed the glass hungrily and gulped down a mouthful. Almost as soon as the vinegar hit his throat, he realized it was not water. Tears flowed into his eyes and he dropped the glass to the floor, coughing and retching pitifully in his agony.

With Shaskof standing behind Pine, Yori pulled the terrified girl to her feet. Stripping off her sweater and bra, Yori slammed her against the wall, the cigar still hanging from his lips.

Laura watched with fascinated horror as Yori removed the cigar from his mouth, flicked the ash to the floor, and sucked it fully alive once more. He slowly brought the lit end towards her left breast. As it approached her, Yori's legs held her firmly in place. Pine leaned forward in horror and she began to sob helplessly. Suddenly, Yori ground the cigar into her breast, just below the wide, red areola. Laura shrieked horrendously, her eyes protruding with terror.

With a bellow of rage, Pine launched himself from the chair towards Yori's back. Laura had fainted, and as she began to slide down the wall, he slammed into Yori. The force of his drive carried the Russian forward, his head smashing into the stone wall. Turning quickly, he reached for Pine, who directed a shattering blow at Yori's neck. Ducking defensively, the Russian caused the punch to miss the jugular and careen off the side of his neck. He grunted with pain and stepped in low. Pine brought the edge of his hands down sharply on the back of the big man's neck, drawing another groan from him. This time Yori dug his fist deeply into Pine's already weakened stomach. Air shot out of him, and before he could recover, he felt a crushing weight on his head from behind.

It was dark and very cold. He was lying against something that vibrated softly and warmly. A wave of pain and nausea passed over him as he tried to sit up.

"Lie still," a voice whispered in his ear. "Don't try to move yet."

Looking up and back, he saw nothing. Everything was black.

"Laura?" he queried softly. "Laura? Where are you?" he called slightly louder.

"Right here." Her voice was very close. Suddenly he realized that he was lying in her arms. It was her naked breast that felt so warm, and the vibrations were the shudderings of her body. He was covered by his jacket and they were lying on his shirt and Laura's sweater.

"Put your sweater back on, Laura. You must be freezing."

"No, Mark," she replied softly. "I can't wear the sweater yet anyway."

Raising himself to a sitting position, he still could see nothing.

"Laura," he said, with growing panic. "I think I'm blind. I can't see a thing."

"They've turned out the lights," she replied, soothing him. "It's too dark to see anything."

"What happened after I attacked Yori?"

"When I came to, you were lying on the ground at my feet. Yori had blood on his face and Shaskof was standing behind you with a boot in his hand.

"After that, they just left us here and went away. The lights went off later."

"Laura," Pine said quietly. "We've got to get out of here before they return."

He crawled on his knees and started fishing through his pockets for something, anything. But aside from a few items that were of no use in the stone room, all he got was a cut on his knee from some of the broken glass that was lying about the floor. When he rose, dizziness hit him again, and he almost fell. Taking his shirt and draping it carefully over his shoulders, he handed her the sweater and threw his jacket over her shoulders. Laura snuggled deeply into the damp garment, thankful for its meager warmth.

For the first time in his life, he was sorry that he did not smoke; he would have given anything for a match or a lighter.

He crawled to the wall, gingerly avoiding broken fragments of glass, and then stood up and reached as far as his sore arms permitted. Then he began to sidle around the room, with his body flush against the wall. At a corner he ran into the protruding wall, and grunted with pain as his burn scraped the cold, lime encrusted stone.

"Are you all right?"

"Yeah . . . sure."

When he felt the steel ring on the wall, recognizing the place where he had been strung up, he dropped to the ground to see if he could find a piece of the glass he had broken that was large enough to be used as a weapon. Running his open palm lightly over the floor, his hand brushed against a small box. It was the box of matches that Yori had used when he had lit his cigar. Hurriedly, and without effect he struck one several times against the emery that coated a side of the box. Then, suddenly, a flame sprang to life. Laura came rushing over to the light.

"I never thought light could be so inviting."

The wooden stick quickly burnt down to a charred wisp, and Pine let it drop. Holding Laura tightly against himself, carefully keeping her left breast away from his body, he kissed her. Pine felt a growl in his stomach; it was a fine time to remember that he was hungry.

23

Pine wasted another match, and took a quick look around the cell in which they were being held captive. He could find no obvious escape route. It appeared that the beating he had received had done him no serious damage, other than to render him stiffer and sorer than before, and the blood he had tasted during the ordeal had come from his nose. Even as he lay there the sharp pains around his chest and ribs began to subside into a dull throbbing. He was adequately fit to effect some degree of self-defense, if necessary, and if not too strenuous. The burns on his back, however, were exceedingly painful, especially when he tried to extend his arms, or when something touched against them. His greatest discomfort, strangely enough, was his increasing hunger.

Checking his watch, he saw that it was almost midnight. Since it was late, he hoped that Shaskof would not continue his interrogation that night, but would wait until morning, allowing him time to recover. If he were given enough time, he might devise some plan of action, although he was not sure exactly where to begin. He was concerned that after his attack on Yori, he would not be let off as easily the next time the maniac worked him over.

Pine assured himself that Laura was seated as comfortably as possible, and took the other for himself. As they sat in the darkness, Pine trying to evolve some plan of escape, they could hear occasional scrapings, as a rat scampered across the chamber. Each time the rattle of tiny nails chattered across the floor, Laura shuddered audibly. Pine tried to keep his arm around her shoulders, but it was too painful, stretching the skin around his burns. Two hours later, he had still not come up with a workable plan, and he began to feel the rise of panic.

Pine walked around the room a few times, feeling the walls and checking the door, but could find neither a way to breach the enclosure, nor to open the locked door.

The cold air had begun to work its way into Pine's body, and his bruises and cuts ached with increasing wrath. His battered body, weak from lack of food, was totally enervated, and his throat, sore from his screaming and irritated by the vinegar he had swallowed, was further aggravated by the raw air.

"You know, Laura," he said. "I might as well be frank with you. I don't think we have much chance of getting out of here. The way I look at it, if we can't escape, Yori will surely kill us both. I have nothing that they want, but they apparently don't believe me. But even if I had something important to tell them, they would never let us get away.

"The point is, we are going to have to try to escape. If we die in the process, it will be quicker and less painful than having to go through another session with that sadist."

Laura shook her head in agreement. Pine decided that as

soon as the others returned he would try to disarm anyone who might have a weapon. If there were no weapons, he would go for Yori and try to get to him. With Yori out of the way, he felt that they had a better chance with the others. But getting Yori would be no simple matter.

As Pine contemplated his offense, there was a clank at the door. Slowly, the great door opened and Boris stepped quickly into the room. He had a package under his arm, and peering into the hall, he partially closed the iron door. There was something about his manner that caused Pine to hesitate.

"Do not make any loud noises," Boris whispered. "They are all sleeping, but one never knows who might come by."

Pine looked closely at Boris in the thin ray of light that entered through the slitted door. The initial shock of the light on his eyes made him realize how helpless he actually would have been if someone had entered with a weapon; it made his plan useless.

"I know that you have not eaten," Boris continued. "I have brought some bread and a small bottle of fruit drink. It was all I could get from the kitchen without it being missed." He handed the bread over. "I do not like to see barbaric treatment, even of prisoners."

The bread was a long French loaf that appeared to be a few days old. It may have been hard and dry, but it was the most luscious meal that Pine could remember having eaten; the fruit juice, although warm, tasted like nectar. Laura, despite her long fast, did not eat much, but drank her share of the juice eagerly.

As Pine shoved crumbly hunks of bread into his mouth, he looked at Boris, who glanced back at the door occasionally.

"Mr. Pine," Boris began before Pine had a chance to question him. "I have brought these things to you because I do not always approve of Shaskof's and Yori's methods. Do not think for a moment that I am your ally. But I do wish you would tell

187

them what they want to know. Yori, as you might imagine, is looking forward to tomorrow."

"I appreciate the food, Boris, but as I told Shaskof, I don't know anything to tell."

"Don't be a fool. I am not here to trap you. Tell them what they want."

Perhaps Boris felt that the other man's condition was so bad that he would not be able to fight, but Pine realized that this might be his only chance. Pine seemed to slip forward groggily in his seat, as if suddenly faint. Boris leaned forward, closer to him, the better to speak. With his feet braced under him, Pine shot upright, bringing the heel of his left hand sharply into Boris's chin. Boris's head snapped back, and Pine swung viciously at his throat with the outer edge of his stiffened right hand. Stumbling on the chair that he had overturned, Pine lost his footing in the dark and came down on top of the Russian. The blow had not struck true, but it had knocked Boris unconscious. Kneeling over the prostrate man, Pine turned him on his back and raised his hand to smash his wind pipe; Laura brough her hands up to her face and turned away.

Pine looked down at Boris and hesitated. He could not kill him in cold blood.

Laura slipped into the sweater, discarding the bra which she found too painful to wear, and they left the cell through the open door.

"I'm glad you didn't kill that man," Laura said. "It would have been so . . . so . . ."

"It would have been the practical thing to do," Pine interrupted, aggravated by his weakness, but relieved by his decision. "The fewer opponents we have the better chance we'll have of getting away."

Boris had carried no weapons, but the key to the doors separating the cellar from the main room upstairs had been in one of his pockets. Pine carefully relocked each door as they passed through. At least Boris would be unable to give them away until he was found in the morning. As they approached the door to Shaskof's study, Pine motioned Laura to stand back. Opening the door a crack, Pine could see that the lights were out. Presuming that nobody would be there in the darkness, he stepped into the room. The warm air felt soothing to his battered body. Laura followed quickly behind him. Walking lightly toward the French doors, Pine checked them to see if they were open and if any guard was on duty outside. Everything was still and the calm seemed incongruous. Turning the handle on the doors slowly, Pine pressed outward and cringed as the entire glass frame rattled noisily.

"Slide it, stupid!" Laura whispered in mild exasperation. She picked her coat from the chair where she had left it earlier and slid it over her shoulders.

Shame-faced, Pine slid the door to the side and it opened with a grinding rumble. Grabbing Laura's arm, he led her out to the slate porch.

"Wait here a minute," he whispered. "I'm going back in to see what I can find in that room."

"Don't be an ass," Laura blurted. "Haven't you got enough trouble without asking for more?"

Pine could not be dissuaded. He did not know where or how far from safety they were, and hoped that he could find a weapon for later.

Lighting a match, Pine looked around the room quickly. He had been amazed by the amount of light the match had shed in the confines of their prison; now it seemed to provide no assistance at all. Pine tried each of the drawers in Shaskof's desk, but they were all locked. Grabbing a letter opener from the tabernet behind the desk, Pine jammed it into the space between the center drawer and the desk top. After prying for a moment, the lock finally gave with a sharp snap.

"Will you come on, already," Laura snorted through the open French doors. "I can't stand this."

"In a minute. Just a minute." Pine retorted, putting the letter opener in his jacket pocket.

There was nothing in the center drawer but a small black book. Flipping through the pages, Pine saw that it contained names and address in several countries, including the United States. There were also cryptic comments after each name, written in what seemed to be some kind of code. Pocketing the book, Pine looked into the other drawers, which now opened easily. There were no weapons in any of them, but Pine found the list of missile sites that had been taken from him.

Shoving the list into his inside pocket, Pine looked around the room again. In the far corner was a safe. The combination locked outer door was ajar and inside, Pine could see a second door. He went to the safe, and dropping on one knee, he saw that the inside door lock was operated by a key. He had seen a key in one of the desk drawers and hoped it was for the safe.

"Will you hurry up?"

"Yes, in a minute. I'll be right out."

Pine rushed back to the desk and after rummaging, found the key. It fit snugly into the lock, and with a well oiled motion, the heavy door opened soundlessly. Rifling through the papers inside, Pine saw documents in Russian, French, German, and other languages that he did not recognize. One of the papers was in English, and contained a diagram of a building with strange symbols at various points on the drawing. Underneath, were a few handwritten notes in Russian. Pine shoved that document into his pocket to keep the list company.

Looking wistfully at the other papers, too many to take with him, Pine made a dangerous decision. Pausing for a moment to listen for any sounds in the house, he went to the telephone and dialed the number of the Embassy. There was a click, and the phone was answered.

Whispering into the receiver and hoping that he could be heard, Pine identified himself.

"Pine," the voice answered. Diver and French had not left the Embassy and had been waiting for just such a call. "Where the hell are you?"

"Diver?" Pine replied. "Thank God! Listen, I don't have much time to speak. I don't know where I am right now. It's a chateau or something out in the country. There's no number on the phone, but maybe you can trace it."

"Yes, yes. Go on." Diver's voice sounded tired.

"There's this safe here with all kinds of information in it that looks important. You've got to get out here as quickly as you can. Laura is with me; I mean Miss Kennedy. We're going to try to get away on foot. Get out here as fast . . ."

Pine paused. The voice on the other end of the line repeated his name anxiously a few times. Pine was not listening to it. Standing at a door, looking into the room, was Yori.

The big Russian switched on the lights and without a word, lunged. Dropping the receiver on the desk top, Pine sidestepped quickly. Yori caught himself and turned his attack back in Pine's direction, chasing him around the desk.

"I told you to hurry. I told you to hurry," Laura repeated over and over again.

Suddenly, in a powerful rush, Yori leaped over the side of the desk and managed to get himself between Pine and his protection. Yori closed carefully on Pine in a crouch with his two hands extended in a fighting position. Pine also dropped into the stance he had learned in the Marines. The two men circled for a moment, then Yori shot a quick jab at Pine's face. Stepping hard to right, then back sharply to the left, Pine threw a straight-armed chop to Yori's heart, using a closed fist. The blow landed squarely and Yori staggered back, losing his balance for a moment. Pine thought that he had broken his hand.

Moving in quickly to gain the advantage, Pine brought the flat edge of his left hand down powerfully on the line between Yori's neck and shoulder. The strength of the slice doubled up the Russian's body. Pine then swung his right fist up into his opponent's face. The punch missed as Yori slid to the side and thrust his rigid left hand deep into Pine's midsection. Pine doubled with pain and felt the edge of Yori's hand come down on the back of his neck. Had he not slipped on the telephone cord as the blow landed, it would have killed him.

Rolling sharply to his left, away from the desk, Pine just missed having the heel of Yori's boot crush his spine. Yori's foot came up again, this time to come forcefully down upon Pine's head. Pine grabbed at the foot as it came, and twisted. At first nothing happened. Then, as if a great tree were being felled, Yori began to go over. Pulling his legs up under him, Pine shot to his feet lifting Yori's leg swiftly into the air. Yori went down like a bag of cement, smashing his head against the desk. Without a second's grace, Yori pulled himself to his feet and flew at Pine's exposed chest. Bracing himself, Pine stepped into Yori and brought his fist into Yori's chin, using the force of Yori's own drive to add momentum to the punch. It was like hitting a block of lead. Without waiting for the vibrations in his right arm to calm, Pine slashed down hard with the edge of his left hand on Yori's shoulder.

The Russian grunted with the blow and doubled over. Pine brought both fists down upon the back of the Russian's neck, and at the same time, brought his right knee up into his face. He heard a sickening crunch, but did not stop to see what had been done. As Yori's body straightened from the force of Pine's knee, he chopped at the exposed throat viciously, using the first two tightly-balled knuckles of his right hand. Yori's eyes bulged and his right hand went out, grabbing at Pine's left ear.

Trying to dodge the hand, Pine ran into a powerful blast from the left that caught him on the side of the neck. Staggering, he stepped back for a moment. Yori followed closely, smashing his right fist into Pine's chest. Falling back onto the desk, Pine rammed his right foot into Yori's stomach and, as Yori bent over and backwards, pressed forward, hitting the Russian with all his strength in the pit of the stomach. Pine could hear the wind go out of the man. Yori grabbed Pine's lapels with both hands; he seemed unable to stop the Russian monster.

Stepping back sharply and clasping his hands firmly together, Pine brought his arms up hard between Yori's hands, which flew apart, taking the left lapel with them. Pine whipped his coupled hands down, crashing their edges into Yori's shoulder blades. The shock forced Yori's head down, and clasping his hands stiffly behind his opponent's neck, Pine again pulled Yori's face into his rapidly rising knee.

Yori's head flew back, spraying the room with blood. Pine again swung hard at Yori's throat. The shot drew a deep groan from within the Russian's chest. Pine chopped down viciously on the bridge of Yori's nose with the edge of his left hand and then, slamming up with the heel of his right hand, drove the broken cartilage deeply into the Russian's brain. Eyes wide, a shocked expression on his face, the silent Russian stood erect for a moment, then toppled.

Laura had stood by the door watching in frightened silence. Now she began to shake.

"Please Mark," she sputtered. "Please come now."

The fight had not taken more than two or three minutes, but that was time enough for the others to have been awakened by the noise. Pine had still not found a weapon, and the phone was lying on the desk, its connection open, a clacking sound issuing from the receiver. But there was no time for him to clean up last minute details.

Joining hands, the two began a mad dash across the lawn

toward a highway which he could see over the low brick wall that bordered the estate. He only hoped that there were no prowling dogs on the grounds.

Looking back at the chateau, Pine could see lights flashing on throughout the building. As they reached the wall, he saw several figures standing at the French doors, looking out in the direction that they had gone. He wondered how long it would take them to catch up.

24

Pine pushed and shoved Laura over the wall and after he scrambled over, they found themselves on a dark road that seemed to stretch for miles in each direction. Along the sides of the road were deep woods and small ditches. He did not know which direction led to Paris, and no signs posted the way. It was quarter to three in the morning.

Crossing to the opposite side of the road, they headed through the woods in the hope of finding a house from which they could get directions and, perhaps, even find a phone. Although he had not broken phone contact back at the chateau, he had no way of knowing whether Diver had been able to trace the call. At any rate, he was certain that he would not meet Diver on the route he would be taking. Laura was beginning to tire, but Pine urged her on, and only after fifteen minutes of struggle through thick underbrush, did they rest.

The woods ended when they came to another road, where they made a right turn. About one hundred yards ahead of them, the road curved sharply to the right. When they came to the curve, they saw a sign indicating that Paris was in the opposite direction, about thirty kilometers distant. Making a quick calculation, Pine figured that he could ordinarily cover the eighteen or nineteen miles in about four-and-a half hours if he hurried and did not pause to rest. In his present condition, he expected that the trip would take closer to six hours, and Laura would not last that long. Laura's high heeled shoes were going to cause her trouble, but Pine suggested that she not remove them because the road had a rough gravel surface.

They had walked for about forty-five minutes toward Paris and were just about to rest, when Pine noticed that the road intersected another a few hundred feet ahead. He suggested that they stop for their rest at the intersection, and he put on a burst of speed. The intersection led into another road of similar construction, and a sign pointed the way to Paris. Twenty-seven kilometers to Paris, the sign threatened.

Across the road, Pine saw a low wall enclosing a field. Looking across it, he recognized the building at the far end. It was the chateau; they had come full circle.

"Look over there, Laura. I don't believe it."

Laura gave a gasp and looked tiredly at him.

"What are we going to do?" she asked.

"We'll just have to keep on going, putting as much distance as we can between us and that place."

"Do you think they'll see us pass?"

"I doubt it," Pine replied. "They're probably out now looking for us in a car. We'll have to stick close to the edge of the road. If we see a car coming, we can dive into the ditch."

Laura began to limp after another thirty minutes. They had travelled at a fair pace, and Pine realized that they would have to rest if they hoped to continue further. Sitting on the wet grass at the side of the road, shielded by a few short scrubby bushes, Pine felt as though he would never be able to rise again. The road had been quiet and Laura asked if he thought that the search for them had ended.

"I don't think so. I do think that they are either ahead of us or went the other way first."

A soft murmuring up the road brought Pine back to attention. Peering between the wild plantings, he could see two men approaching from the direction in which they had been going. The men, who were walking on opposite sides of the roadway and speaking to each other in Russian, were beating the shrubbery with staves and flashing lights into the bushes. Putting his hand to Laura's lips, Pine rose to one knee, and leaned forward. He motioned Laura to lie flat on the ground, and began to feel around under the bushes for a stone or some other object to use as a weapon. The voices were coming closer.

The men were not searching with particular care, but the thin October foliage remaining on the sparse roadside vegetation would not protect them from the most cursory glance. Pine did not believe he could defeat both men in his present condition.

Putting his hand absently into his pocket, Pine found the letter opener that he had used to jimmy the desk lock. He fished the blade out, and tested the edge on his thumb. It was as keen as the edge of a baby's crib, but it had a sharp point. The blade was made of cast iron, and the handle had a good grip. He hoped that it would not break off if he had to use it.

Pine tossed a stone high over the heads of the two Russians. It fell on the other side of the road, deep in the foliage. The searchers stopped talking at once and turned away from Pine's hiding place to face the opposite side of the road. The man on Pine's side walked to the middle of the highway, drawing a gun from his pocket. He was about ten feet away. The other man walked into the woods a few paces, and made a hushed comment to his compatriot. Pine threw a second stone that fell a few feet deeper into the bushes, and about a dozen feet further down the road. The men turned, exposing their backs to Pine.

Stepping out as quietly as he could, Pine raced the ten feet to the closest Russian. At the last minute, the man began to turn. Before he could react, Pine had slapped his hand across the man's mouth and driven the point of the letter opener deeply into his back. The blade did not go in easily; Pine could not pull it out again. The gun fell from the Russian's hand and clattered on the ground.

The other Russian, who had been walking deeper into the scrubby field, turned quickly when he heard the gun fall, and for an instant could not see Pine hidden behind his associate. Then, giving a yell, he brought his weapon up and fired a shot. The bullet thudded into the man whom Pine held, driving them both back a step. Dropping to the ground with the dead man, Pine slithered toward the gun. The other Russian fired three more rounds at him, one of which again struck the dead man, the other two chirping off the roadway, showering Pine with gravel. Pine found the pistol, an automatic, and hoped that the fall had not jammed it.

Rolling to his stomach, holding the gun with two hands and resting upon his elbows, Pine took aim and fired. His first shot hit the other man, who had remained standing, square in the face. The Russian brought his hands to his head and fell over backwards without a sound. Grabbing the first man's flashlight, Pine ran to the other's side and took his gun. He had a neat hole in the center of his forehead.

Conscious of the noise that the shooting had made, Pine ran back to the man who was lying in the road, and pulled him into the ditch at the side of the highway. When he returned to Laura, she was crying softly.

"Oh Mark," she stammered. "How can these things happen? Do you realize that you've killed five men in the past few days, Mark? Five men!" She started to sob again.

Pulling the shaking girl to her feet, Pine put his arm around her shoulders and hugged her to him. Although her arms rubbed against his burns and sent a shock of fire through his back, the comforting contact compensated for the pain.

Moving as quickly as possible, the two fugitives continued on until Laura felt that she would drop. She had removed her shoes, and had been walking on the wet grass in the shoulder to avoid the rough pavement. Her feet were frozen, but she was too tired to care.

As they came to a tight curve, a car, running without headlights, came speeding up the road from the opposite direction. Diving out of the way, Pine knocked Laura on her back into the bushes. Spinning around, the gun already in his hand, he saw the car, a Fiat, screech to a halt and accelerate back at them, squealing as the rubber was abraded from the tires. Had Pine's reactions been quicker, he probably would have shot without waiting, but the combined affect of exhaustion and his physical state held his trigger finger for a moment.

"Pine!" The word was a sharp command. "It's me, Diver!"

Pine almost sank to his knees with relief. The cavalry had arrived in the nick of time. Sinking down against the car's fender, Pine looked into the vehicle and saw Diver and King. King had a submachine gun across his lap. Pine was glad that he had not fired; King might have used the thing. Laura was walking to the car and Pine helped her into the back seat. Following her in, Pine stretched back and smiled at his rescuers.

"Diver," Pine said happily. "If I didn't think it would make Laura jealous, I'd kiss you."

"Kiss him," Laura said from behind closed eyes.

"Now, what's going on up at that chateau? We weren't sure

that you'd still be willing to cooperate. It's lucky we put a tracer on the line. We started tracing as soon as the call came through." Diver turned up the car's heater a little, and Pine began to drift.

"Don't fall asleep on us now, Pine. Come on, keep 'em open."

"You guys must be kidding." Pine found it difficult to move his lips articulately as the warmth of the vehicle seeped into him. "What do you want to know?"

"We've got the address and we know which place it is. What we don't know is how many of them there are, and what kind of armament they have."

"Well, I can't help you too much there," Pine replied. "I know that there are still at least two. I just killed two others about fifteen minutes ago. But there may be more. I just don't know."

"We've got more men coming. We went ahead because of you two. I guess it might be wise to wait for the others to arrive."

Pine told them what had happened to him and Laura since their last meeting. He was just finished with a description of the documents in the safe when, looking over their turned heads, he saw two headlights approaching from the direction from which they had just walked.

"Hey," he exclaimed, sitting upright. "Look what's coming up ahead. If it's who I think it is, Mohammed is not going to have to make that long trip to the mountain."

Diver and King turned back simultaneously to see the headlights, approaching now at a greater speed. Slipping the car quickly into reverse, Diver shot back in a steep turn. Then shifting into first, he dropped in the clutch and floored the accelerator. The little car spun around to the direction from which it had come, and began to creep forward with appallingly slow acceleration. Pine could see the headlights gaining on them from the rear with incredible speed. Diver passed the car through second, third and finally fourth, winding out the engine at each change of gears.

Pine could see that the speedometer already read about ninety kilometers per hour, but the car behind was doing a lot better than sixty miles an hour. The little Fiat crept along, gaining speed slowly. Pine watched the needle crawl past one hundred kilometers, one-ten, one-twelve. The needle began to quiver at about one-fifteen, close to seventy miles an hour. What the hell were those bastards driving, he wondered as their car closed on them. King looked back at the couple in the back seat and shrugged.

"You two had better get down so I can get in a clean shot. We'll never outrun them in this crate."

Suddenly, a hail of bullets crashed through the back window of the little car. The glass sprayed over everyone in the car, and the chatter of a submachine gun behind them kept up its rhythm a few seconds. Taking careful aim through the shattered glass, King pulled off a few rounds from his gun. He missed. The car that had been following them sped up beside the Fiat and forced it off the road into a ditch. Pine worked his way over Laura and flung the door open, pulling her out of the car on top of him. Slamming the door, he rolled Laura under him, as he pulled out one of the automatics he had taken from the Russians he had killed.

King and Diver followed him out of the car almost as quickly. Diver had a nasty looking Luger gripped tightly in his hand.

"I knew that I should have brought some grenades," he said.

The rest of his comment was lost in the machine gun fire that started up from the other side of the road. Pine noticed that the opposition had been driving a shiny, new Stingray.

25

The sky had become substantially lighter since Diver and King had come. Pine hoped it was an omen. After the Russians had forced Diver's car off the highway, they had pulled up some distance in front of it, and had jumped out, carrying submachine guns. When the four Americans had taken cover, guns drawn, the two Russians had leaped into a shallow gully on the opposite side of the road. Now they were dug in, and because of the grade of the roadway, they were firing on the Americans from a slightly higher vantage point.

Stealing around the rear of the car, Pine could see the muzzles of the opposing guns poking out from behind a ridge. Diver and King had slipped farther down the road to the front of their car, and were firing into the ditch where the Russians were lying. Laura was burrowed deeply in a trench behind the Fiat, her attention riveted to Pine.

The Russians were making broad sweeps with their guns, and Pine could hear the lead slugs slamming into the body of the car that was his shelter. At any moment, he expected to feel one smash into his own body. Keeping his head low, he sighted on an area immediately below the muzzle of the nearest Russian's weapon. He pulled off three quick shots, and he ducked back as gunfire turned in his direction. Diver continued the barrage from his Luger. King ripped short blasts from his machine gun, trying to conserve ammunition and to keep the barrel of the weapon cool.

"How many rounds have you got left?"Diver called over to Pine.

"I'm not sure," Pine replied, checking the clip in his gun and in the one stashed in his pocket. "About five shots," he finally said.

"That's great," Diver commented. "I have this one clip, and King has only one additional clip for the Tommy gun. We'd better make each shot count."

Looking over the terrain, Pine could see no better position from which to shoot. In the Russians' present location, they could be fired upon all day without causing any damage.

"Stop firing for a moment," Diver called to the others. "We can't hit them where they are, but they can't reach us either, without moving. Let them waste their ammunition for a while."

"The question is, how long it will be before some more of them come?" King said. "How far up the road is the chateau?"

"I'm not sure how far we came in the Fiat," Pine answered, "but it couldn't be more than a few miles or so."

"French ought to be here soon," Diver added. "I hope he makes it."

The Russians had fired for a few minutes after the Americans stopped, and then they too ceased firing. It was a stalemate. Pine saw a head peek up and took a fast shot. He saw the man jerk his head back, after emitting a short yelp. How much damage he had done, he did not know. After a short return volley in Pine's direction, all firing ceased again.

Every few minutes, Pine looked down the road towards Paris, hoping to see some sign of French and his reinforcements. He also cast occasional glances in the opposite direction, expecting to see unwelcome company arriving in aid of the Russians. The Stingray had been left running, and was now idling, with a heavy cough so that Pine could not hear if any cars were coming.

As he was watching one of the Russians, who seemed to be moving slowly along the trench to get into a better position from which to shoot, he heard a low rumble from the Paris direction. In the distance, he saw a blur of motion around a bend. As he peered intently under cover of the Fiat, a car became visible, approaching at a high rate of speed. With one eye on the Russians and the other on the oncoming vehicle, Pine called to Diver, who was closer to the Stingray, and could not hear the nearing vehicle.

"Diver, old buddy," he said. "It looks like the Marines have landed." Pine nodded up the road. Diver looked towards the onrushing car, squinting to make out the occupants in the low light of morning.

"I sure hope it's French," he said, "and not just another vehicle using the highway."

"What the hell is French doing, coming by himself, if that's him?" King wanted to know. "He should have several cars with him.

The car was closer now, a late model Citroën. The car slowed as it approached the parked vehicles, and one of the Russians began firing on it. Swerving sharply to the side and dangerously close to the ditch where the Russians were lying, the Citroën braked and three men piled out, all carrying weapons.

Throwing themselves on the ground behind their car, they returned the Russians' fire. A man with a Browning automatic rifle was sighting carefully and taking well aimed shots. From their position on the highway, the new arrivals looked directly down upon the Rusians, and the fight was over in less than a minute. One of the Russians had been shot in the arm, and was coming out with his good arm held over his head. The second Russian had been killed.

Diver and King rose and walked over to the three men, who stood waiting with their handcuffed prisoner. Pine assisted Laura, who held his arm tightly. He did not recognize any of the new men and presumed that they were some of French's Embassy people and that French had either decided to stay behind or come up later. He was not particular who his rescuers were; he was only too glad to have them join the party.

One of the men was speaking with Diver in a low voice as Pine approached them. Pine noticed that he had a slight French accent, and that he was introducing the other men to Diver.

". . . and Cambert you already met, Percy," the Frenchman finished as Pine walked up.

"Well, I don't know how you found out about us, Pomey," Diver said, "but we're grateful that you came when you did."

The three men ignored the thanks and fastened their gaze primarily upon Pine.

"And you are the notorious Monsieur Pine, I presume," Pomey stated.

"That's me," Pine replied.

"This is Pomey, Cambert and Dubois," Diver said. "They're with French Intelligence." Diver gave Pine a look that said "watch what you say."

"We've been looking for you, Monsieur Pine."

"What exactly do you want with me?"

Pine had moved next to Diver and in front of King. As they spoke, King tried to move away from the little grouping, and off to the side. As he moved, Pomey brought up his weapon, and pointed it at them, motioning King back into the fold.

"Please forgive me, gentlemen ... and lady." He had a resigned look on his face, as if he were resolved to do something that he hated doing. "But I have my orders regarding Monsieur Pine." Dubois disarmed each of the Americans, and dropped the weapons in a pile behind Pomey.

Pine looked around incredulously. He could not understand what was going on between these men, but it seemed as if he was once again the pivot.

"Would somebody mind explaining to me what's happening?" Pine inquired, taking a step closer to the Frenchmen.

"Do not try anything courageous, Monsieur Pine," Pomey instructed. "As you can see, my friends also have their weapons directed at you. Tell me, what did you find at the Russians' chateau?"

Pine confronted Pomey. He knew that the French police were interested in his involvement with the two dead Germans at Rue de Vaugirard, and he also knew that French Intelligence was interested in the list that he had obtained there, but he had no idea that they would go to such extremes to get it.

"Well, er, nothing." he said hesitantly, recalling Diver's nonverbal admonition. "I was more concerned with getting out than with taking anything.

"I think you had better let one of my associates search you, just the same," Pomey said.

Cambert started walking to Pine, while Pomey stepped back, keeping his gun aimed between the three American men. Laura was standing in the background again, unable to do anything, and feeling helpless.

"If you think that I'm going to let this guy touch me, Mister, you've got another think coming," Pine said, turning toward Cambert off. "You take another step, Mac, and I'll show you how we make pâté in America."

"Do not be foolish, Pine," Pomey retorted. "If you resist, we will shoot you first and search you afterwards."

"You've got to be kidding. You'd never get away with it. There are witnesses. What kind of bullshit is this anyway?"

"Monsieur Pine." Pomey spoke seriously. "You are a man who is suspected of murder by the police. We arrived and found you with all these dead bodies and you resisted arrest. Your associates aided you. There was a gun battle and you were all killed. It is very simple to explain; how were we to know that they were American agents working with the Embassy?"

Pine realized that Pomey must have been prompted by his superiors, who obviously considered the matter important enough for such extreme steps. There was nothing that he could do, and it appeared that he had little to lose. If Pomey got the papers, Pine's role would be ended. Diver could worry about getting them back for the Americans. Pine started to reach into his inside jacket pocket.

"What do intend to do with us after you have what you came for, Pomey?" Diver quickly injected.

"That is an embarrassing question, my friend. I do not like my job at times."

"You're going to shoot us, aren't you?" Laura said.

"Ma'amselle," Pomey said remorsefully. 'I cannot tell you how difficult this is for me. But I must follow my orders. It is a war that we are engaged in. I did not know that you would be here. My orders include everyone."

"You won't get away with this, of course," Diver said. "You know that Washington will know the truth."

"I don't think that will be a problem," Pomey replied.

"Your country will spend a few weeks kicking the issue around, and then it will be dropped. Just like the Berlin Wall, the American airmen who were shot down in East Germany some ten years ago, Laos. It's all the same."

"What do you hope to gain by this, Pomey? I don't understand."

"Do you think I know what my country's goals are? I merely follow orders, just like you. They tell me nothing except what I am supposed to do, and I don't ask questions. It is hard enough doing my job when I know nothing. It is a matter of National security."

Pomey snapped back the chamber of his machine gun, and pointed it in the general direction of the Americans. As they braced themselves a loud engine noise was heard behind the Americans. Pomey turned to see a Bentley bearing down on them. Turning to look at the welcome intruders, Pine could see that Boris was driving the car, and that Shaskof was next to him.

The men leaped to the side as the Russians' car barrelled past them, squealing to a stop a few yards ahead. The Bentley spun around, jammed into gear again, and aimed at the Americans.

When the car had first sped through the center of the standing party, Pine had leaped to the side of the road where the Fiat was parked. He still had the other automatic in his jacket pocket. Drawing the gun, he fired at Dubois. The first shot hit him in the leg; a second went through his heart.

Diver and King had been separated from Pine by the Bentley, and found themselves on the same side of the road as Pomey and Cambert. Rushing the two Frenchmen, the Americans grabbed for their weapons.

By the time Pine had fired his second shot the Bentley had come about and was aimed directly for him. Scrambling back up the road, he stumbled into the Russian who had surrendered to the French. Grabbing him by his belt with one hand, and by his jacket collar with the other, Pine heaved him at the onrushing Bentley. The car jammed its brakes, but slammed into the Russian's chest.

In the confusion, Laura had leaped to Diver and King's side of the road. Running into the woods to get out of the line of fire she saw Pine running down the road, chased by the gear-grinding Bentley. When the car struck the Russian's body, she heard the crash of the collision, but could not see who had been hit.

Pine ran with the Bentley bearing down upon him. Turning sharply back in the direction from which he had been coming, he dodged the car, this time hearing a shot fired from the vehicle. Dropping close to the ground he raced back past the already turning automobile, and toward the still idling Sting-ray. Laura saw him run past and made a dash for him.

Pine shouted at her to drop, and threw himself to the ground as a sharp pain cut through his scalp. The grazing bullet only stunned him for a moment, but it was long enough for Boris to gain ground. Pine looked up to see the car practically on top of him. As the Bentley came on, he heaved himself into the ditch to the right.

Leaping to his feet, Pine dashed for the Stingray, and slid behind the wheel. The Bentley started another run at him, but this time he was trapped in the little fiberglass vehicle. Hearing the chatter of a machine gun, Pine turned to see Diver cutting down the two remaining French agents. As he watched Diver spin to bring the gun to bear on the Bentley, he slipped in the clutch, and spun his rear tires viciously until the little car leaped into the road. The Bentley was no more than three feet behind him as he passed to second and raised to third, the Stingray responding with incredible power and speed.

With a roar, the Corvette accelerated, and just as the front bumper of the Bentley made contact with the rear quarter of the smaller car, the distance between the two began to widen. Pine heard three shots cut through the Stingray's soft fiberglass body. He hoped that they had not pierced the fuel tank, which was only quarter full. Finally dropping her into fourth gear, Pine kept the pedal pressed to the floor and heard the deep growl of the mighty engine as it propelled the light bodied automobile faster and faster. He knew that the Bentley could move, but it had neither the acceleration nor the top speed of the American racing car. As Pine sped away, he saw Laura in his rear view mirror, standing next to King and behind Diver, both of whom were firing at the receding Bentley.

26

Pine directed his full attention to the road ahead. His speedometer registered ninety-five miles an hour.

His general fatigue and the rubbery feeling in his legs made Pine distrust his reactions at high speeds. In addition, the bullet that had grazed his scalp, had given him an acute headache, and blood was running slowly into his left eye. He was worried that the Russians would get within gun range and hit one of his tires. At his speed, it would be fatal. Depressing the accelerator, he watched the needle climb to one hundred.

The Bentley was still close on his tail. The original fifty feet that had separated them, had dwindled to about thirty feet, and Pine was beginning to wonder what they had under the hood. No more than fifty feet ahead there was an extremely sharp turn. He chopped the shift down to third, and hit the brakes hard. The little car chattered all over the road, and when he hit the turn at about seventy-five miles an hour, he ran off the road and into the shoulder. The Stingray bumped itself back onto the highway and continued to accelerate. The road was straight for several miles, and Pine had his opportunity to put some distance between him and his pursuers.

With one eye on the rear-view mirror, Pine watched while the Bentley safely made the turn, noting that it was now, perhaps, half a mile back; Boris, knowing the road, had slowed and taken no chances on the sharp turn. The Bentley again had begun to pick up speed, and Pine was shocked to see that it was beginning to creep up on him. He wondered if the British vehicle had been fitted with a supercharger.

The fork in the road came up so quickly that he did not have a chance to choose his direction. It was all he could do to brake sufficiently to prevent the car from sluing off the highway and into the ditch on the side. Reducing his speed, Pine fought for control of the powerful machine.

The quality of the pavement also began subtly to change. No longer was it smooth blacktop, but it had become a broken, badly patched surface with chuckholes every few yards. After hitting a few, he further reduced his velocity. The road began to describe various S curves, and the condition of the surface continued to deteriorate rapidly. Pine could see the Bentley, with its heavier body and softer shocks, bouncing dangerously behind him. It had closed the distance that it had lost, and was now within firing range. Two shots rang out, but neither hit the car as it rocked down a sharp incline.

At the bottom of the slope, the road turned sharply to the left, and Pine, arms braced tightly, pulled hard against the wheel, and bounced the car through the turn. For a moment, he thought he would roll over, but the low center of gravity held the car level. Pine now found himself on a totally un-paved roadway. The Bentley had navigated the turn with an

212

expertise that Pine had to admire. A few more shots came from behind, but again, none of them made contact with his vehicle.

After about half a mile, the road began to rise steeply. Pine drove towards the apex of the slope, wildly steering through a series of sharp turns. Still inclining, the crumbling roadway cut through a rocky area along a ledge on a steep cliff. The road was less than one-and-a-half car widths, and at the speed he was going, a single slip would be fatal. Blood from his scalp wound continued to drip into his eye, making it hard to concentrate on the roadway, and perspiration had begun to bead on his forehead. The edge of the road was directly abutting a sheer drop of several hundred feet, and there were no guard rails. If he hit the jagged cliff wall he would be propelled over the precipice by the force of contact. There was little room for error.

The Bentley seemed to pop over the top of the hill, having also made the sharp turns without mishap. Although the distance between the two cars had lengthened, the Bentley was still close. The road was too dangerous for Pine to sustain the speed at which he had been driving. Pine hoped that the precarious road would end before the Bentley could reach him.

The roadway was curving to the left, keeping the Bentley hidden by the cliff-face. Perspiration mixed with blood was practically pouring into his left eye. Blinking rapidly, he tried to clear his vision without removing his hands from the wheel. The possibility of another car coming from the opposite direction on the narrow road was something he did not want to think about.

Suddenly, the Bentley's grill appeared in the rear-view mirror from around the curve. The car could not have been more than twenty feet behind, and was bearing down fast. He could see Boris's face in the mirror. It was tense and deep in concentration. Pine began to feel a rush of panic, and was hard pressed to keep his eyes on the road.

The Bentley was no more than ten feet behind him, and a few shots careened off the roof. It moved closer as the slope of the hill began to decrease, and it lightly touched the rear of the Corvette. For a frightening moment, Pine thought that he would be run off the road. Again the big car tapped the Vet on the rear bumper. Pine wanted to increase his speed, but he was going as fast as he could with any control.

The gas gauge read nearly empty, and Pine, not knowing how accurate it was, could imagine the hungry engine, sucking up the last dregs of fuel and sludge from the tank. The Bentley was a bit farther behind, but as he slowed, he could see the distance shortening.

Suddenly, a few hundred yards ahead, Pine could see that the roadway ended. A rustic stone wall ran along the opposite side of the crossroad. Envisioning what would happen if he hit the wall, and momentarily forgetting about the Bentley behind him, he jammed on his brakes as the intersection loomed closer. The Bentley, coming up behind him, tried to swerve away from the rapidly slowing rear of the Corvette. There was a horrendous grating of tires on loose soil, and a deafening crash as the English car grazed the rocky face of the cliff. Bouncing off at seventy miles an hour, the big car slammed into the rear of the Stingray, tearing off its right rear quarter, and jamming the crushed fender into Pine's right rear tire. The tire was punctured instantly, and the Vet lurched to the right, threatening to throw itself and its passenger over the edge of a twenty foot drop.

Using all the strength left in his arms, Pine fought the wheel and charged into the face of the cliff, tearing off the left front fender and smashing the windshield. Scraping along the wall, the Stingray shuddered to a stop; Pine turned off the ignition, his face white with shock and exhaustion.

The Bentley was squirming all over the dirt road, throwing vast waves of sand and gravel into the air. With a twisting motion the British import seemed to lift itself and leap over the edge of the crag. For a moment, there was complete silence; then a terrific crash broke the calm. A second or two later, Pine heard a tinkling of glass.

Pine pushed his way out of the passenger side of his car. Running to the edge of the road, he saw the Bentley lying on its side on the rocks below. Boris's head had been pushed through the front windscreen. Shaskoff was lying beneath the car, the roof bisecting his middle. With a shock, Pine realized that Shaskof was not yet dead; he could see the body writhing and squirming under the weight of the broken automobile.

Pine took a few steps over the edge of the declivity. Suddenly, a flame licked up at the rear of the car and quickly spread over the ground around it. Shaskof screamed in agony. Almost as if it were a signal, the entire Bentley was engulfed in a billowing shroud of fire that was followed, a few seconds later, by a muted explosion. The force of the blast knocked Pine to his knees on the slope, and he started to slide down the incline. Catching himself on a low shrub, he scurried up the hill to the road above, and climbed over its lip. The heat of the flames was intense, even at a distance. As echoes of the explosion receded, two deep thuds followed and flames leaped thirty feet into the air leaving a thin trail of black smoke and soot behind.

Walking wearily towards the intersection, Pine felt the tension of the past few hours falling away. He could barely keep his eyes open, and the fresh cool air seemed to lull rather than awaken him. He decided to sit by the sign post that indicated direction toward Paris, until someone came along and gave him a lift. Dropping heavily onto the ground, he was alseep within seconds.

The sharp blast of a car horn woke him with a start. Looking up, he saw a man standing beside a Peugeot. Laura was fast alseep in the back seat. Behind the Peugeot, Pine could see Diver stepping from the Citroën that the French agents had used. A little bald man with a black bag, who had scurried out of the Peugeot, was now walking over to Pine with the stranger.

"Hell of a place to bed down for a night," Diver said with a grin. "I'd like you to meet Mr. French. He finally made it."

Pine grinned back at them, too tired to reply. The little man checked Pine over, cleaned some blood from his face, and nodded to Diver and French.

"I guess you've got a few things to tell us?" Diver said.

"Perhaps you could begin by telling me what happened back there," Pine replied, nodding back up the road.

"Well," Diver began, "French drove out from Paris with another carload of men and the doctor. When he reached the place where we were waiting, we left Laura with the Doc and a guard and went to the chateau to check it out. You were right about the stuff in the safe; it was pretty hot. French wanted us to wait with Laura, hero that he is," Diver continued with a smile, "but we felt that he might need some extra protection. Meanwhile, the doctor gave Laura a sedative."

Diver helped Pine to his feet and led him to the Peugeot and to Laura.

"There's going to be a stink when the French learn about Pomey, Cambert, and that other guy they sent out. But we'll cool them off when we show them copies of some of the documents we found back there," Diver continued.

"You mean, that after all that, we're going to give those bastards what they wanted in the first place?" Pine was astounded.

"We're not going to show them anything," King interposed, stepping out of the Citroën with a briefcase. "We're

216

only going to show them the proof we obtained of their intervention in North Vietnam. The Russians had copies of the French-Vietnamese agreements in about seven languages."

Diver and King returned to the Citroën, and Pine entered the Peugeot with French. He looked into the back seat where Laura was sleeping, and smiled.

"She sure looks peaceful," Pine said. "I could use some of that sleep myself."

"Don't get too comfortable yet," French said. "Did you happen to pick up any papers yourself back at the chateau?"

Pine reached into his inside jacket pocket and withdrew the list of Soviet missile sites, the other document that he had taken from the safe, and the black book.

"With all the excitement, I completely forgot about these."

French looked out of the car window towards the Citroën, and placed the documents in his own jacket pocket.

"What about the charges against me?" Pine queried.

"We'll have those dropped in no time, after we get back to Paris," French said. "You'll be a free man, and can return to New York on the next plane if you wish. In fact, I suspect that the French authorities will appreciate it. You won't be their favorite person for a while."

Pine got into the back seat of the Peugeot and rested Laura's head on his shoulder. He was asleep before the car started to roll.

A few days after their return to Paris, Diver made reservations for Pine and Laura to return to New York. Personally escorting them to the airport, Diver waited with them in the lounge.

"You know," Pine said. "After all we went through getting that stuff you wanted, I almost forgot to give French the junk I had taken from the chateau."

Diver smiled as he lit a cigarette.

"No problem," he said. "French gave us the papers."

"And the black book," Pine added.

"Which book was that?" Diver asked. "We found several things that would qualify as books."

"You know," Pine said, looking up. "The little black book, like a small phone book. It contained names, addresses and some cryptic notes."

"Oh yes," Diver replied. "That one."

After the two Americans had boarded the plane, Diver went to a phone and made three calls.

February, 1979

Combined News Services
Washington—A spokesman for the State Department has announced that Parris French, a senior staff member, shot himself early yesterday evening at his offices here.

Mr. French, who had served with the Paris Embassy for many years, and who was presently serving as a foreign economic advisor, was known to have been suffering from an undisclosed illness.

It was reported that he was pronounced dead on arrival at Walter Reed Hospital.

The storm had left over six inches of snow on the hilly roads of Tappan, and Pine had decided to spend the day at home with Laura and the kids. After a late breakfast, he went into his study, and flipped idly through the morning paper. An article on page 23 caught his eye, just as Laura came in.

"Say honey," he said. "Do you remember that fellow French who was with the Embassy in Paris when we met?"

"Sure," she said. "Why?"

"There's an article in the paper about some guy named French who killed himself," Pine continued. "I think it might be him."

"Huh," she said. "No kidding. Let's see." She glanced at the paper. "Imagine that," she said, looking at Pine with raised eyebrows. Pine closed the paper.

"How about taking Rob sledding?" she said.